THE ADVENTURES OF KATIE AND JAINU

KSHITIJ JAIN

INDIA · SINGAPORE · MALAYSIA

Contents

Chapter 1

The Beginning of an Unexpected Adventure

The forest was thick with the scent of pine and damp earth, a place where sunlight filtered through the canopy in dappled patches. For as long as he could remember, Jainu had called this forest his home. It was a place of peace, where the worries of the outside world could not reach him. He spent his days wandering its many paths, listening to the rustle of leaves and the songs of birds, finding solace in the simplicity of nature.

But today was different. Today, the forest felt alive in a way it hadn't before, as if it was waiting for something to happen. Jainu couldn't shake the feeling that something—someone—was about to cross his path and change everything.

Jainu wasn't the kind of person who sought out adventure. At 27 years old, he was content with his quiet life, preferring the company of trees and animals to that of people. He was a bit of an introvert, finding it easier to express himself through the work he did with his hands—carving wood, tending to the small garden behind his cabin—than through words.

That morning, as he walked down the familiar path toward the stream where he often went to fish, he noticed something unusual. The birds were quieter than usual, the air seemed heavier, and the forest itself felt as if it were holding its breath.

As Jainu approached the stream, he saw her. A woman stood by the water, her back turned to him as she knelt down to dip her fingers in the cool current. She had a satchel slung over one shoulder, and her short brown hair was slightly disheveled, as if she had been traveling for a while. She was humming a tune he didn't recognize, something light and whimsical, that seemed to blend perfectly with the sounds of the forest.

Jainu paused, unsure of whether to approach. He hadn't seen another person in the forest for weeks, and the sight of her both intrigued and unsettled him. But something about her drew him in, like a moth to a flame.

The woman must have sensed his presence because she turned around suddenly, her eyes wide with surprise. For a moment, they simply stared at each other, both caught off guard.

"Oh!" she exclaimed, quickly standing up and brushing off her tunic. "I didn't see you there! I'm sorry if I'm trespassing."

Jainu shook his head, finding his voice at last. "No, you're not trespassing. This forest is free for anyone to explore."

The woman smiled, a bright and warm smile that reached her eyes. "Well, that's a relief! I'm Katie, by the way. Katie Willow. I've been traveling for a few days now, just exploring the area. And you are?"

"Jainu," he replied, feeling a little self-conscious. "I live nearby, in a cabin just a little ways back."

Katie's eyes lit up with curiosity. "You live here? That's amazing! I've never met anyone who lives in the middle of a forest. What's it like?"

Jainu wasn't sure how to answer. "It's... peaceful. Quiet. I like it."

Katie nodded, her expression thoughtful. "I can imagine. There's something magical about this place, don't you think? It's like the forest is alive."

Jainu found himself agreeing with her, though he wasn't sure why. There was something different about today, something that made him feel as though the forest was more than just trees and earth. It was as if the forest itself had brought them together for a reason.

Katie didn't seem like someone who would enjoy living in solitude. There was an energy about her, a liveliness that was contagious. She radiated a sense of adventure, and Jainu could tell that she was someone who thrived on new experiences.

"So, what brings you here?" Jainu asked, trying to make conversation.

"I'm on an adventure," Katie said, her eyes sparkling. "I've always loved exploring new places, and when I heard about this forest, I just had to come and see it for myself. There's something about the unknown that just calls to me, you know?"

Jainu nodded, though he couldn't quite relate. He had always been content with what he knew, with the familiar. The idea of venturing into the unknown was daunting to him, but he could see the excitement in Katie's eyes, the way her entire being seemed to light up at the thought of discovering something new.

They fell into a comfortable silence after that, the kind that felt natural rather than awkward. Jainu found himself relaxing in Katie's presence, something he hadn't expected. There was something about her that put him at ease, despite her exuberant personality.

As they stood by the stream, watching the water flow by, Katie suddenly turned to him with a mischievous grin. "How about a race?"

Jainu blinked, taken aback. "A race?"

"Yeah!" Katie said, already bouncing on the balls of her feet, ready to take off. "Let's see who can get to the big oak tree over there first!"

Before Jainu could respond, Katie took off running, her laughter echoing through the trees. For a moment, Jainu just stood there, stunned. Then, with a shake of his head and a small smile, he started after her.

He wasn't sure why he was doing this—he hadn't run just for the fun of it in years—but there was something infectious about Katie's enthusiasm. It made him feel lighter, freer, as if he were shedding some invisible weight he hadn't even realized he was carrying.

Katie was fast, but Jainu had spent years navigating the forest, and he knew the shortcuts. He darted through the trees, his feet finding purchase on the uneven ground as if by instinct. The wind rushed past him, and he felt a thrill of exhilaration that he hadn't felt in a long time.

When he reached the big oak tree, Katie was already there, leaning against the trunk with a triumphant grin on her face. "Beat you!" she said, breathless but clearly pleased with herself.

Jainu couldn't help but laugh, a sound that felt strange in his throat but also right. "You got a head start," he pointed out, though there was no real complaint in his voice.

"Maybe," Katie said, her eyes twinkling. "But a win's a win!"

Jainu shook his head, still smiling. "You're something else, you know that?"

Katie shrugged, unbothered. "I like to have fun. Life's too short to be serious all the time."

Jainu couldn't argue with that. He had spent so much of his life being serious, focused on the practicalities of living in the forest. But being around Katie made him realize that there was more to life than just surviving. There was room for fun, for laughter, for silly races and spontaneous moments.

As they caught their breath, Katie turned to Jainu, her expression more serious now. "So, what do you do out here all by yourself?"

Jainu hesitated, unsure of how to answer. He wasn't used to talking about himself, especially not to someone he had just met. But there was something about Katie that made him want to open up, to share a piece of himself.

"I carve wood," he said finally. "I make things—bowls, utensils, sometimes little figurines. It's something I've always enjoyed."

Katie's eyes lit up with interest. "Really? That's amazing! I'd love to see some of your work."

Jainu felt a flush of pride at her words. It wasn't often that he received compliments on his work—mostly because there was no one around to give them. "I have some pieces back at the cabin if you want to see them."

"I'd love to," Katie said, her enthusiasm genuine. "Lead the way!"

As they walked back to Jainu's cabin, the conversation flowed easily between them. Katie asked questions about his life in the forest, about the things he had seen and experienced, and Jainu found himself answering more freely than he had expected.

When they reached the cabin, Jainu led Katie inside and showed her his workshop. It was a small space, filled with the scent of wood shavings and the tools of his trade. Jainu picked up a small wooden figurine he had been working on—a raccoon, its features carefully carved to capture the animal's playful nature.

Katie's eyes widened as she took in the intricately carved figure. "Jainu, this is incredible! You're really talented."

Jainu felt a warmth spread through him at her praise. "Thank you," he said, a little shyly. "I enjoy it. It's calming, you know?"

Katie nodded, her eyes still on the figurine. "I can see that. There's something special about creating something with your own hands, isn't there? It's like you're putting a piece of yourself into it."

Jainu hadn't thought of it that way before, but he realized that she was right. Each piece he carved was a reflection of who he was, of the time and care he put into it. It was a way of expressing himself, of leaving a mark on the world.

As they continued to talk, Jainu found himself opening up more and more, sharing stories of his life in the forest, of the things he had learned and the challenges he had faced. Katie listened intently, her curiosity insatiable, and Jainu found himself enjoying the conversation more than he had expected.

It was strange, how easily they had fallen into a rhythm, as if they had known each other for years rather than just a few hours. Jainu couldn't remember the last time he had felt so at ease with someone, so comfortable in their presence.

As the afternoon wore on, they moved outside, sitting on the porch of Jainu's cabin as the sun began to set. The sky was painted in shades of orange and pink, and the air was filled with the sounds of the forest winding down for the night.

Katie leaned back, her eyes closed as she took a deep breath of the cool evening air. "This place is beautiful, Jainu. I can see why you love it here."

Jainu nodded, his gaze drifting over the familiar landscape. "It is. It's home."

Katie opened her eyes and turned to him, a thoughtful expression on her face. "Do you ever get lonely out here? I mean, I love being in nature, but I think I'd miss being around people."

Jainu considered her question carefully. "Sometimes," he admitted. "But I've gotten used to it. The forest... it's like a friend. It keeps me company."

Katie smiled softly, as if she understood. "I get that. But I'm glad we met. It's nice to have someone to share this with."

Jainu felt a warmth in his chest at her words, a feeling of connection that he hadn't realized he had been missing. "Me too," he said quietly.

They sat in companionable silence for a while, watching as the sky darkened and the stars began to appear. There was something magical about the forest at night, something that made the world feel both vast and intimate at the same time.

Katie was the first to break the silence, her voice soft and contemplative. "Do you believe in magic, Jainu?"

The question took him by surprise. "Magic?"

"Yeah," Katie said, her eyes fixed on the stars above. "You know, the kind of magic that makes the impossible possible. The kind that turns ordinary moments into something extraordinary."

Jainu thought about it for a moment. "I'm not sure. I've never really given it much thought."

Katie turned to him, her eyes sparkling with that same curiosity that had drawn him to her in the first place. "I think there's magic in the world. It's in the little things, like the way the light filters through the trees or the sound of the wind in the leaves. It's in the connections we make with others, in the way we can find joy in the simplest moments."

Jainu wasn't sure if he believed in magic, but he couldn't deny that there was something special about the day he had spent with Katie. It was as if the forest itself had come alive, as if it had been waiting for this moment, for them to find each other.

As the night deepened, Katie eventually decided it was time for her to find a place to set up camp. She declined Jainu's offer to stay at his cabin, insisting that she was used to sleeping under the stars. They said their goodnights, and Katie promised to come by in the morning before they continued exploring the forest together.

As Jainu watched her disappear into the trees, he felt a strange mix of emotions—excitement, curiosity, and something else he couldn't quite name. Katie had brought something new into his life, something that made him feel alive in a way he hadn't felt in years.

He went inside and stoked the fire, letting the warmth fill the cabin as he prepared for bed. But even as he settled down for the night, his mind was buzzing with thoughts of the day's events, of the unexpected friendship he had found in the middle of the forest.

As he drifted off to sleep, he couldn't help but wonder what tomorrow would bring. The forest was full of secrets, and with Katie by his side, he felt ready to uncover them all.

The next morning, Jainu woke up earlier than usual, the excitement of the previous day still fresh in his mind. The forest outside his cabin was bathed in the soft light of dawn, and the air was crisp and cool. He dressed quickly, his movements filled with energy and purpose, eager to see what the day would bring.

After a quick breakfast, he stepped outside, taking a deep breath of the fresh morning air. The forest was alive with the sounds of birds singing and leaves rustling in the breeze. It was a beautiful morning, the kind that made him feel grateful to be alive.

Jainu made his way down the familiar path to the stream, where he and Katie had agreed to meet. As he walked, his mind was filled with thoughts of what they might discover together, of the mysteries that awaited them in the depths of the forest.

When he reached the stream, he found Katie already there, sitting on a rock by the water's edge. She looked up as he approached, her face lighting up with a bright smile.

"Morning, Jainu!" she called out, her voice filled with cheer.

"Morning, Katie," he replied, returning her smile. "Ready to start our adventure?"

"Absolutely!" Katie said, standing up and stretching. "I've been thinking about it all night. I have a feeling we're going to find something amazing today."

Jainu felt a thrill of excitement at her words, and he nodded in agreement. "Me too. Let's get started."

They set off together, following the path that wound deeper into the forest. The air was cool and crisp, filled with the scents of pine and earth. Sunlight filtered through the canopy, casting dappled shadows on the ground as they walked.

Katie kept up a steady stream of conversation as they moved through the forest, her voice lively and animated. She talked about her travels, the places she had seen, and the people she had met. Jainu listened with rapt attention, his mind filled with images of distant lands, of mountains and oceans, of cities bustling with life.

"You've seen so much," Jainu said, a hint of envy in his voice. "I've never left this forest. It's always been enough for me."

Katie turned to him, her eyes sparkling with curiosity. "Why? Don't you ever want to see what else is out there? The world is so big, so full of possibilities."

Jainu shrugged, his gaze drifting to the trees that surrounded them. "The forest is my home. It's where I feel most at peace. Out there… it just seems too chaotic, too overwhelming."

Katie smiled softly, as if she understood. "I get it. But sometimes, it's good to step out of your comfort zone, to see what the world has to offer. You might be surprised at what you find."

Jainu didn't respond immediately. He was lost in thought, contemplating her words. He had always been content with his life, finding solace in the simplicity of nature. But Katie's words stirred something within him—a longing, a curiosity he hadn't felt in years.

As they continued deeper into the forest, the path became narrower, the trees closer together. The underbrush was thick with ferns and moss, and the air was filled with the earthy scent of damp soil. The sounds of the forest surrounded them, the rustle of leaves, the chirping of birds, the distant call of a hawk.

Jainu found himself relaxing, the tension he had felt earlier melting away in the tranquility of the forest. The sounds, the scents, the sights—it was all familiar, all comforting. And yet, there was something different, something new, about this journey. The presence of Katie by his side, the sense of purpose that filled him, made everything seem more vibrant, more alive.

After a while, they came across a small clearing, the sunlight pouring down through a break in the canopy. The ground was covered in soft grass, dotted with wildflowers. It was a peaceful spot, and Katie suggested they take a break.

They sat down on the grass, the warmth of the sun on their faces. Jainu leaned back, propping himself up on his elbows as he looked around. The clearing was beautiful, the kind of place that made him feel connected to the world, to the earth beneath his feet.

Katie was quiet for a moment, her gaze thoughtful as she looked around the clearing. Then she turned to Jainu, her expression serious. "Jainu, what do you think we'll find? Do you think there really is something hidden in this forest?"

Jainu considered her question, his mind turning over the possibilities. "I don't know," he said finally. "But I think it's worth looking. There's something special about this place, something that feels... different."

Katie nodded, as if she had expected that answer. "I feel it too. That's why I was drawn here in the first place. There's something about this forest, something magical. I just know it."

Jainu looked at her, seeing the determination in her eyes, the conviction in her voice. It was hard not to believe her, hard not to feel the same sense of excitement, of possibility.

As they sat there, in the quiet of the clearing, Jainu felt a sense of calm settle over him. The doubts, the fears that had been swirling in his mind, began to fade. There was a purpose to this journey, a reason for everything they were doing. And for the first time in a long while, Jainu felt truly at peace.

When they were ready to continue, they stood up and resumed their journey. The path ahead was uncertain, and there were no guarantees that they would find anything at all. But the thrill of the unknown, the promise of discovery, was enough to make them eager to begin.

For the rest of the day, they explored the forest, following paths and trails that Jainu had never taken before. They climbed hills and crossed streams, discovering hidden glades and ancient trees. The forest seemed to open up to them, revealing its secrets little by little.

At one point, they came across a fallen tree, its massive trunk blocking the path. The tree was old, its bark rough and weathered, its roots twisted and gnarled. It was clear that it had been there for a long time, a silent sentinel in the heart of the forest.

Katie walked up to the tree, running her hand along its rough surface. "This tree must have seen so much," she said, her voice filled with reverence. "Imagine the stories it could tell if it could speak."

Jainu nodded, feeling the same sense of awe as he looked at the tree. There was something majestic about it, something that made him feel small in the presence of such ancient life.

They spent a few moments in silence, paying their respects to the fallen giant, before continuing on their way. The path was difficult, the underbrush thick and tangled, but they pressed on, driven by the excitement of what they might find.

As the afternoon wore on, the forest began to change. The trees grew taller, their branches intertwining overhead to form a dense canopy that blocked out most of the sunlight. The air grew cooler, and the sounds of the forest seemed to fade, replaced by a heavy silence.

Jainu felt a shiver run down his spine, a sense of unease creeping in as they ventured deeper into the forest. There was something different about this part of the woods, something that made him feel as if they were being watched.

Katie seemed to sense it too, her steps slowing as she looked around, her expression serious. "This place feels... different," she said softly. "Like we've crossed into another world."

Jainu nodded, his senses on high alert. "We should be careful. I don't like the feeling of this place."

But despite the unease, there was a part of him that was intrigued, that wanted to see what lay ahead. The forest was full of mysteries, and he couldn't help but feel that they were on the verge of discovering something important.

They continued on, moving cautiously through the dense undergrowth. The trees were ancient, their trunks thick and twisted, their roots snaking across the ground like the fingers of some great unseen creature. The air was heavy with the scent of damp earth and decaying leaves.

At one point, they came across a narrow stream, its water dark and still. The stream was bordered by moss-covered rocks, and the water was so clear that they could see the pebbles at the bottom. It was a beautiful, if eerie, sight.

Katie knelt by the stream, dipping her fingers into the cool water. "This place is strange," she said, her voice hushed. "But it's also beautiful. There's something about it that feels... otherworldly."

Jainu nodded, feeling the same sense of wonder. The forest was full of surprises, and this place, with its ancient trees and silent stream, felt like a world unto itself, separate from the rest of the forest.

As they continued on, the forest grew even darker, the canopy above blocking out most of the light. The path was narrow and winding, and they had to move carefully to avoid tripping over the roots that crisscrossed the ground.

After what felt like hours, they finally emerged into another clearing, this one larger than the first. The clearing was ringed by massive trees, their branches forming a dense wall of foliage that seemed to close them off from the rest of the world.

In the center of the clearing was a large stone, half-buried in the ground. The stone was covered in moss and lichen, its surface weathered by time. It looked ancient, as if it had been there for centuries, untouched by the passage of time.

Katie approached the stone, her eyes wide with awe. "This is it," she whispered, her voice filled with reverence. "This is what we were meant to find."

Jainu felt a shiver run down his spine as he looked at the stone. There was something about it, something that made him feel as if they were standing on sacred ground. The air was heavy with a sense of power, of something ancient and unseen.

Katie reached out to touch the stone, her fingers brushing against its rough surface. The moment her skin made contact, a soft glow began to emanate from the stone, a pale blue light that seemed to pulse with life.

Jainu gasped, taking a step back in shock. The light was mesmerizing, beautiful and strange, and it filled the clearing with an otherworldly glow.

Katie didn't move, her hand still resting on the stone, her eyes wide with wonder. "Jainu," she said softly, her voice trembling. "This is it. This is the magic we were looking for."

Jainu didn't know what to say, his mind racing with thoughts of what this could mean. The stone, the light, the feeling of power in the air—it was all overwhelming, and he couldn't help but feel a sense of awe mixed with fear.

"What do we do now?" he asked, his voice barely above a whisper.

Katie turned to him, her eyes shining with excitement. "We explore. We find out what this is, what it means. This is just the beginning, Jainu. There's so much more to discover."

Jainu nodded, feeling the same sense of determination. The adventure they had started was far from over, and now, with this discovery, it felt as if they were on the brink of something incredible.

They spent the rest of the day in the clearing, examining the stone and the surrounding area. The light continued to glow softly, casting a gentle light over the clearing. Jainu and Katie took turns touching the stone, feeling the strange energy that seemed to emanate from it.

As the sun began to set, casting long shadows across the clearing, they finally decided to head back. The walk back through the forest was filled with a sense of anticipation, of excitement for what lay ahead. The stone, the light, the feeling of power—it was all a mystery, and they were eager to unravel it.

When they reached the spot where their paths diverged, Katie turned to Jainu with a smile. "We've got a lot of work ahead of us, Jainu. But I know we're going to find something amazing."

Jainu returned her smile, feeling the same sense of excitement. "I can't wait to see what we discover."

With a final wave, Katie disappeared into the trees, her figure quickly swallowed by the darkness. Jainu stood there for a moment, listening to the sounds of the forest, before turning and making his way back to his cabin.

As he walked, his mind was filled with thoughts of the adventure that lay ahead. The forest, which had always been his refuge, was now a place of mystery and possibility, and he was ready to embrace it.

When he finally reached his cabin, Jainu felt a sense of calm settle over him. The fire was still burning in the hearth, casting a warm glow over the room. He sat down in his usual spot, staring into the flames as they danced and flickered.

For the first time in a long while, Jainu felt a sense of purpose, a drive to do something more than just exist. The forest, which had always been his refuge, was now a place of mystery and adventure, and he was ready to embrace it.

As he drifted off to sleep that night, Jainu's dreams were filled with images of distant lands, of hidden treasures and magical places. And always, by his side, was Katie, her laughter ringing out like a melody, guiding him through the darkness.

The next day arrived with the sun shining brightly through the trees, casting a warm golden light over the forest. Jainu awoke with a sense of eagerness, the memories of the previous day still vivid in his mind. He was excited to see what new discoveries awaited him and Katie as they delved deeper into the mysteries of the forest.

After a quick breakfast, Jainu stepped outside his cabin, breathing in the fresh morning air. The forest was alive with the sounds of birds singing and leaves rustling in the breeze. It was a beautiful day, the kind that filled him with energy and anticipation.

He made his way to the stream where he and Katie had agreed to meet. As he walked, he couldn't help but think about the glowing stone they had found the day before. The memory of its soft, pulsing light filled him with a sense of wonder and curiosity. What was its purpose? Why had it been hidden away in the depths of the forest for so long?

When Jainu reached the stream, Katie was already there, sitting on a large rock with her legs crossed. She was humming a tune, her eyes closed as she enjoyed the peacefulness of the morning. As soon as she heard Jainu approaching, she opened her eyes and greeted him with a bright smile.

"Morning, Jainu!" she called out, her voice filled with cheer. "Ready for another day of adventure?"

"Morning, Katie," Jainu replied, returning her smile. "I've been looking forward to it."

They set off together, following the path that led deeper into the forest. The air was cool and crisp, filled with the scents of pine and earth. Sunlight filtered through the canopy, casting dappled shadows on the ground as they walked.

Katie was in high spirits, her excitement palpable. She talked animatedly about the possibilities that lay ahead, her voice full of enthusiasm. Jainu found himself getting caught up in her energy, feeling the same sense of anticipation.

"So, what do you think the stone is?" Katie asked as they walked. "Do you think it's some kind of magical artifact?"

Jainu considered her question. "It could be. The way it glowed when you touched it… it felt like it was alive somehow, like it had a purpose."

Katie nodded, her eyes shining with excitement. "Exactly! I think there's something special about it, something that's connected to this forest. We just have to figure out what it is."

Jainu agreed. The forest had always been a place of mystery, and the discovery of the stone had only deepened that sense of intrigue. He was eager to uncover its secrets, to learn more about the magic that seemed to be woven into the very fabric of the forest.

As they continued on their journey, they came across a series of strange markings carved into the trunks of several trees. The symbols were intricate and unfamiliar, and they seemed to form a path that led further into the woods.

Katie's eyes widened as she examined the markings. "This is incredible! It's like a trail, leading us to something."

Jainu studied the symbols, his curiosity piqued. "It's definitely a trail. But where does it lead?"

"There's only one way to find out!" Katie said with a grin, already moving ahead to follow the markings.

Jainu chuckled and hurried to catch up with her. Despite his natural caution, he couldn't help but feel a thrill of excitement at the prospect of uncovering more secrets of the forest.

The trail led them through a dense part of the woods, where the trees grew close together and the underbrush was thick with ferns and moss. The air was cooler here, and the sounds of the forest seemed to be muffled, creating an eerie, almost reverent silence.

After following the trail for what felt like hours, they finally emerged into a small clearing. In the center of the clearing stood a large stone altar, similar in appearance to the glowing stone they had found the day before. The altar was covered in moss and lichen, and it was surrounded by a ring of ancient-looking trees.

Katie approached the altar cautiously, her eyes wide with wonder. "Jainu, look at this! It's like a shrine or something."

Jainu nodded, feeling a sense of reverence as he looked at the altar. There was something powerful about this place, something that made him feel as if they were standing on sacred ground.

Katie reached out to touch the altar, her fingers brushing against the rough surface. As soon as her skin made contact, the same soft, pulsing light they had seen the day before began to emanate from the stone.

Jainu gasped, taking a step back in awe. The light was mesmerizing, casting an ethereal glow over the clearing. It felt as if the very air around them was charged with energy, as if the forest itself was alive and aware of their presence.

"This is amazing," Katie whispered, her voice filled with wonder. "I've never seen anything like it."

Jainu couldn't find the words to respond. The sight of the glowing altar left him speechless, filled with a mixture of awe and curiosity. What was the purpose of this place? What kind of magic was at work here?

As they stood there, the light from the altar seemed to grow brighter, filling the entire clearing with its glow. The air around them began to hum with energy, and Jainu could feel a strange warmth spreading through his body.

"Katie," he said, his voice trembling slightly. "I think something's happening."

Katie turned to him, her eyes wide with excitement. "I feel it too. It's like the forest is trying to tell us something."

Before Jainu could respond, the ground beneath their feet began to tremble. The trees around the clearing rustled as if caught in a strong wind, though the air was still. The light from the altar grew even brighter, almost blinding in its intensity.

Jainu instinctively reached out to grab Katie's hand, holding on tightly as the ground continued to shake. The air was thick with energy, and he could feel his heart pounding in his chest.

Then, as suddenly as it had begun, the trembling stopped. The light from the altar dimmed, returning to its soft, pulsing glow. The forest was still once more, and the air was filled with a sense of calm.

Katie and Jainu stood in silence for a moment, both trying to process what had just happened. The energy that had filled the clearing moments ago had left them both feeling exhilarated and slightly disoriented.

"What was that?" Katie asked, her voice hushed.

"I don't know," Jainu replied, still holding her hand. "But whatever it was, I think it was important."

Katie nodded, her eyes filled with determination. "We need to find out more. There has to be a reason why this is happening."

Jainu agreed. The forest was full of mysteries, and they had only just begun to scratch the surface. There was something powerful at work here, something that they were meant to discover.

As they stood in the clearing, Jainu couldn't help but feel a deep connection to the forest, a sense that he was part of something much larger than himself. The magic of the forest had always been there, just beneath the surface, waiting for the right moment to reveal itself.

And now, with Katie by his side, Jainu felt ready to embrace whatever challenges lay ahead. The adventure they had started was far from over, and he was determined to see it through to the end.

They spent the rest of the day exploring the area around the altar, searching for any clues that might help them understand what they had just experienced. They found more markings on the trees, symbols that seemed to be part of a larger pattern, but they couldn't decipher their meaning.

As the sun began to set, casting long shadows across the clearing, they decided to make their way back to Jainu's cabin. The walk back through the forest was filled with a sense of anticipation, of excitement for what they might discover next.

When they reached the cabin, they were both exhausted but exhilarated. The day had been filled with unexpected surprises, and they were eager to continue their exploration the next day.

After a quick dinner, they sat together on the porch, watching as the stars began to appear in the night sky. The air was cool and crisp, and the forest was alive with the sounds of crickets and owls.

Katie turned to Jainu, her expression thoughtful. "Do you think we'll ever figure out what's going on in this forest?"

Jainu considered her question. "I think we will. It might take time, but I believe we're meant to find the answers."

Katie smiled, her eyes filled with determination. "I hope so. There's so much more to discover, and I can't wait to see what we find."

Jainu couldn't help but feel the same sense of excitement. The forest was a place of mystery and wonder, and he was eager to uncover its secrets.

As the night grew darker, they both began to feel the weight of the day's adventures. They said their goodnights, and Katie went to set up her sleeping bag under the stars, refusing Jainu's offer to stay in the cabin.

Jainu watched her for a moment, feeling a deep sense of gratitude for her presence in his life. She had brought something new and exciting into his world, something that made him feel alive in a way he hadn't felt in years.

As he settled down for the night, Jainu's thoughts were filled with images of the day's discoveries, of the glowing altar and the mysterious symbols on the trees. He couldn't wait to see what tomorrow would bring.

And as he drifted off to sleep, he knew that whatever lay ahead, he was ready to face it, as long as Katie was by his side.

The next morning dawned with a sky painted in soft hues of pink and orange. Jainu woke up feeling more refreshed than he had in a long time, the events of the previous day still vivid in his mind. He quickly dressed, eager to begin the day's exploration with Katie.

After a quick breakfast, he stepped outside to find Katie already up, packing her gear with the same enthusiasm that had marked her every action since they met. She looked up and waved as soon as she saw him.

"Morning, Jainu!" she called, her voice full of energy. "Ready for another day of adventure?"

"Morning, Katie," Jainu replied with a smile. "I've been looking forward to it."

They set off together, following the path that wound deeper into the forest. The air was cool and crisp, filled with the scent of pine and earth. Sunlight filtered through the canopy, casting dappled shadows on the ground as they walked.

Katie was in high spirits, chatting animatedly about the possibilities that lay ahead. Jainu found himself getting caught up in her excitement, feeling the same sense of anticipation as they delved deeper into the mysteries of the forest.

"I've been thinking about the symbols we saw yesterday," Katie said as they walked. "I think they might be some kind of map, leading us to something important."

Jainu nodded thoughtfully. "That makes sense. The way they were arranged, it did seem like they were pointing us in a specific direction."

"Exactly!" Katie said, her eyes shining with excitement. "We just need to figure out how to read them."

Jainu agreed. The symbols had been intricate and unfamiliar, but he had a feeling that they were key to unlocking the secrets of the forest. He was eager to see where they would lead.

As they continued on their journey, the forest around them grew denser, the trees towering overhead and the underbrush thickening. The air was cooler here, and the sounds of the forest seemed to be muffled, creating an eerie, almost reverent silence.

After following the path for what felt like hours, they finally emerged into a small clearing. In the center of the clearing was another stone altar, similar to the one they had found the day before.

This one, however, was different—it was larger, and the symbols carved into its surface were more elaborate.

Katie approached the altar cautiously, her eyes wide with wonder. "Jainu, look at this! It's like the one we found yesterday, but even more intricate."

Jainu nodded, feeling a sense of reverence as he looked at the altar. There was something powerful about this place, something that made him feel as if they were standing on sacred ground.

Katie reached out to touch the altar, her fingers brushing against the rough surface. As soon as her skin made contact, the same soft, pulsing light they had seen the day before began to emanate from the stone.

Jainu gasped, taking a step back in awe. The light was mesmerizing, casting an ethereal glow over the clearing. It felt as if the very air around them was charged with energy, as if the forest itself was alive and aware of their presence.

"This is incredible," Katie whispered, her voice filled with wonder. "It's like the forest is trying to communicate with us."

Jainu couldn't find the words to respond. The sight of the glowing altar left him speechless, filled with a mixture of awe and curiosity. What was the purpose of this place? What kind of magic was at work here?

As they stood there, the light from the altar seemed to grow brighter, filling the entire clearing with its glow. The air around them began to hum with energy, and Jainu could feel a strange warmth spreading through his body.

"Katie," he said, his voice trembling slightly. "I think we're on the right track. Whatever this is, it's important."

Katie nodded, her eyes filled with determination. "We need to find out more. There has to be a reason why this is happening."

Jainu agreed. The forest was full of mysteries, and they had only just begun to scratch the surface. There was something powerful at work here, something that they were meant to discover.

As they stood in the clearing, Jainu couldn't help but feel a deep connection to the forest, a sense that he was part of something much larger than himself. The magic of the forest had always been there, just beneath the surface, waiting for the right moment to reveal itself.

And now, with Katie by his side, Jainu felt ready to embrace whatever challenges lay ahead. The adventure they had started was far from over, and he was determined to see it through to the end.

They spent the rest of the day exploring the area around the altar, searching for any clues that might help them understand what they had just experienced. They found more markings on the trees, symbols that seemed to be part of a larger pattern, but they couldn't decipher their meaning.

As the sun began to set, casting long shadows across the clearing, they decided to make their way back to Jainu's cabin. The walk back through the forest was filled with a sense of anticipation, of excitement for what they might discover next.

When they reached the cabin, they were both exhausted but exhilarated. The day had been filled with unexpected surprises, and they were eager to continue their exploration the next day.

After a quick dinner, they sat together on the porch, watching as the stars began to appear in the night sky. The air was cool and crisp, and the forest was alive with the sounds of crickets and owls.

Katie turned to Jainu, her expression thoughtful. "Do you think we'll ever figure out what's going on in this forest?"

Jainu considered her question. "I think we will. It might take time, but I believe we're meant to find the answers."

Katie smiled, her eyes filled with determination. "I hope so. There's so much more to discover, and I can't wait to see what we find."

Jainu couldn't help but feel the same sense of excitement. The forest was a place of mystery and wonder, and he was eager to uncover its secrets.

As the night grew darker, they both began to feel the weight of the day's adventures. They said their goodnights, and Katie went to set up her sleeping bag under the stars, refusing Jainu's offer to stay in the cabin.

Jainu watched her for a moment, feeling a deep sense of gratitude for her presence in his life. She had brought something new and exciting into his world, something that made him feel alive in a way he hadn't felt in years.

As he settled down for the night, Jainu's thoughts were filled with images of the day's discoveries, of the glowing altar and the mysterious symbols on the trees. He couldn't wait to see what tomorrow would bring.

And as he drifted off to sleep, he knew that whatever lay ahead, he was ready to face it, as long as Katie was by his side.

The next morning, they set out again, determined to follow the trail of symbols they had found the day before. This time, they were more focused, their goal clear. They wanted to understand the magic of the forest, to uncover its secrets and learn its history.

The path they followed led them to another clearing, this one larger than the last. In the center stood a massive stone archway, covered in the same intricate symbols they had seen before. The archway was ancient, its stones weathered by time, but it was still standing strong, as if it had been waiting for them all this time.

Katie approached the archway cautiously, her eyes wide with awe. "Jainu, look at this! It's incredible. What do you think it is?"

Jainu shook his head, unable to tear his eyes away from the archway. "I'm not sure. But it feels important, like it's a gateway to something."

Katie nodded, her expression thoughtful. "Do you think it's a portal? Like in the stories?"

Jainu considered her question. "It's possible. The forest is full of magic, after all. Maybe this archway is a doorway to another part of the forest, or even another world."

Katie's eyes sparkled with excitement. "That would be amazing! We have to find out."

Before Jainu could respond, Katie stepped forward and reached out to touch the archway. As soon as her fingers brushed against the stone, the symbols began to glow, filling the clearing with a soft, pulsing light.

Jainu watched in awe as the light spread across the archway, illuminating the symbols and filling the air with a sense of energy. The ground beneath their feet began to tremble, and the air around them seemed to hum with power.

"Katie, be careful!" Jainu called out, his voice filled with concern.

But Katie didn't seem to hear him. She was completely focused on the archway, her eyes wide with wonder as the light continued to grow brighter.

Then, with a sudden burst of energy, the light flared, and a doorway appeared in the center of the archway. The doorway was filled with a swirling mist, and Jainu could see faint shapes moving within it, as if the doorway led to another world entirely.

Jainu felt a shiver run down his spine as he stared at the doorway. It was both beautiful and terrifying, filled with the promise of adventure and the unknown.

"Katie," he said, his voice trembling slightly. "I think this is it. This is what we've been looking for."

Katie turned to him, her eyes shining with excitement. "I know! This is incredible, Jainu. We have to go through. We have to see what's on the other side."

Jainu hesitated, his heart pounding in his chest.

The idea of stepping through the doorway into the unknown was both exhilarating and terrifying. But he knew that Katie was right. They had come this far, and they couldn't turn back now.

"Okay," he said finally, his voice steady. "Let's do it."

Katie grinned and took his hand, giving it a reassuring squeeze. "Ready?"

Jainu nodded, taking a deep breath. "Ready."

Together, they stepped through the doorway, the mist swirling around them as they crossed the threshold into whatever lay beyond.

For a moment, everything was a blur. Jainu felt as if he was floating, the world spinning around him in a whirlwind of colors and light. Then, with a sudden jolt, they landed on solid ground.

Jainu blinked, trying to clear his vision as he looked around. They were standing in a forest, but it was different from the one they had just left. The trees were taller, their trunks wider and their leaves a deep, vibrant green. The air was filled with the scent of flowers and the sound of birds singing, and the sunlight filtering through the canopy was warm and golden.

"Jainu, look at this place!" Katie exclaimed, her voice filled with awe. "It's like a paradise."

Jainu nodded, still taking in the sights around him. The forest was beautiful, almost otherworldly in its perfection. It felt like they had stepped into a dream, a place where everything was brighter, more alive.

But as they stood there, taking in the beauty of their surroundings, Jainu couldn't shake the feeling that they weren't alone. There was something watching them, something hidden in the shadows of the trees.

"Katie," he said quietly, his eyes scanning the forest. "Do you feel that?"

Katie turned to him, her expression curious. "Feel what?"

Jainu hesitated, unsure of how to explain the sense of unease that had settled over him. "I'm not sure. But it feels like… like we're being watched."

Katie frowned, her eyes narrowing as she looked around. "I don't see anything. But you're right, something does feel off."

They stood in silence for a moment, both of them on high alert as they listened to the sounds of the forest. The birds were still singing, and the wind rustled through the leaves, but there was something beneath it all, a presence that was just out of sight.

Then, without warning, a figure stepped out from behind a tree, its movements fluid and graceful. It was a tall, slender creature, with skin the color of bark and eyes that glowed with an inner light. It moved silently, as if it was part of the forest itself, and it fixed its gaze on Jainu and Katie with an intensity that made Jainu's heart skip a beat.

For a moment, they simply stared at each other, the tension in the air thick and palpable. Then the creature spoke, its voice soft and melodic, like the rustling of leaves in the wind.

"Who are you, travelers?" it asked, its eyes never leaving theirs. "Why have you come to this place?"

Jainu swallowed, his mouth suddenly dry. "We… we came through the doorway," he said, his voice trembling slightly. "We're explorers. We didn't mean to intrude."

The creature tilted its head slightly, as if considering his words. "You are not intruders," it said finally. "But you are not of this world. You have crossed a threshold, and now you stand in a place where few have dared to tread."

Katie stepped forward, her curiosity overcoming her fear. "Where are we?" she asked, her voice steady. "What is this place?"

The creature regarded her for a moment before answering. "This is the heart of the forest, the place where the magic of the land is strongest. It is a place of great power, and it is protected by those who dwell here."

Jainu felt a shiver run down his spine at the creature's words. The heart of the forest—a place of magic and power. It was more than he had ever imagined, and he couldn't help but feel a deep sense of awe and respect for the place they had found.

"What should we do?" Jainu asked, turning to Katie. "Should we leave?"

Katie shook her head, her eyes fixed on the creature. "No. We've come this far, Jainu. We need to learn more about this place. We need to understand the magic that's here."

The creature seemed to approve of her determination, nodding slightly as it regarded them both. "You are welcome to stay," it said. "But be warned—this place is not without its dangers. The magic here is powerful, and it can be unpredictable. You must tread carefully."

Jainu nodded, understanding the gravity of the situation. They were in a place unlike any other, a place where the rules of the world they knew no longer applied. But they were here now, and there was no turning back.

"Thank you," Jainu said, his voice sincere. "We'll be careful."

The creature nodded once more before turning and disappearing back into the forest, its movements as silent as before. Jainu and Katie stood in silence for a moment, both of them processing what had just happened.

Finally, Katie turned to Jainu, her eyes filled with excitement. "Can you believe this, Jainu? We've found something incredible. We're in the heart of the forest!"

Jainu nodded, still feeling a mixture of awe and trepidation. "It's amazing," he agreed. "But we need to be careful. This place is powerful, and we don't fully understand it yet."

Katie nodded, her expression serious. "You're right. But that's why we're here—to learn, to explore. And I can't wait to see what we find."

Jainu couldn't help but share her excitement. The heart of the forest was a place of magic and mystery, and they were standing at the threshold of an incredible adventure. Whatever lay ahead, he knew that they were in it together, and that gave him the strength to face whatever challenges might come their way.

As they began to explore the heart of the forest, Jainu couldn't shake the feeling that they were being watched. But it wasn't a threatening presence—it was more like the forest itself was observing them, curious about the strangers who had entered its domain.

The trees here were even taller and more ancient than those in the outer forest, their branches intertwined to form a dense canopy that let in only dappled light. The ground was covered in a thick layer of moss, soft underfoot, and the air was filled with the scent of flowers and herbs.

As they walked, they came across a series of clearings, each one more beautiful than the last. In one, they found a small pond, its surface as smooth as glass, reflecting the sky above. In another, they discovered a grove of trees with bark that shimmered like silver in the sunlight.

But it wasn't just the beauty of the place that captivated them—it was the sense of magic that seemed to permeate everything. The air was alive with energy, and Jainu could feel it humming just beneath the surface, like a heartbeat.

"This place is incredible," Katie whispered, her voice filled with wonder. "I've never felt anything like it."

Jainu nodded, his own senses heightened by the magic of the forest. "It's like the forest itself is alive, watching us, guiding us."

As they continued to explore, they found more signs of the ancient magic that lay hidden in the heart of the forest. They came across a ring of stones, each one carved with intricate symbols that glowed faintly in the dim light. They found a tree with leaves that shimmered like gold, and when they touched it, they felt a warmth spread through their bodies, as if the tree was sharing its energy with them.

But as much as they were captivated by the beauty and magic of the forest, they couldn't forget the warning they had received. The heart of the forest was a place of power, and they needed to be cautious.

As the day wore on, they decided to set up camp in a small clearing by a stream. The water was crystal clear, and they could see fish swimming lazily beneath the surface. The air was cool and refreshing, and the clearing was bathed in the soft light of the setting sun.

They built a small fire and sat together, enjoying the warmth and the sense of peace that surrounded them. It was a perfect moment, and for a while, they simply sat in silence, taking it all in.

As the night grew darker, they lay down on their sleeping bags, staring up at the stars that twinkled through the canopy above. The sounds of the forest surrounded them—the rustling of leaves, the chirping of crickets, the distant hoot of an owl.

"Katie," Jainu said softly, breaking the silence. "I'm glad we're doing this together."

Katie turned her head to look at him, a soft smile on her lips. "Me too, Jainu. I couldn't imagine doing this with anyone else."

They fell silent again, the warmth of the fire and the magic of the forest lulling them into a peaceful drowsiness. And as they drifted off to sleep, Jainu felt a deep sense of contentment. He was exactly where he was meant to be, and whatever challenges lay ahead, he knew that he and Katie would face them together.

Chapter 2

Into the Unknown

Jainu awoke with the first light of dawn filtering through the trees, the cool morning air brushing against his face. He took a deep breath, the scent of the forest filling his lungs, and for a moment, he simply lay there, savoring the peace and tranquility of the heart of the forest.

Beside him, Katie was still asleep, her breathing slow and steady. Jainu watched her for a moment, a soft smile on his lips. There was something about her presence that brought a sense of comfort and companionship he hadn't realized he was missing until now.

Careful not to wake her, Jainu quietly got up and began to prepare for the day. He fetched water from the nearby stream and started a small fire to warm up some food. As the fire crackled softly and the smell of cooking filled the air, Katie stirred and opened her eyes.

"Morning," she said with a sleepy smile, stretching her arms above her head. "You're up early."

"Morning," Jainu replied, handing her a cup of warm tea. "Figured I'd get things started. We've got a big day ahead of us."

Katie took the cup with a grateful nod and sipped the tea, the warmth spreading through her. "Thanks, Jainu. You're right—there's so much more to explore."

After a quick breakfast, they packed up their camp and set off once more, following a narrow path that led deeper into the forest. The air was cool and crisp, filled with the scents of pine and earth, and the sunlight filtering through the canopy cast dappled shadows on the ground.

The heart of the forest was a place of wonder, and as they walked, they marveled at the beauty that surrounded them. The trees here were ancient, their trunks wide and gnarled, and their leaves shimmered with a soft, ethereal light. The underbrush was thick with ferns and moss, and the ground was carpeted in a lush green that seemed to glow in the soft light.

As they walked, Jainu couldn't shake the feeling that they were being watched. But it wasn't an ominous feeling—instead, it felt as if the forest itself was observing them, curious about the strangers who had entered its domain.

"Do you feel that?" Jainu asked quietly, glancing at Katie.

Katie nodded, her expression thoughtful. "It's like the forest is alive, isn't it? Like it's watching us."

Jainu nodded in agreement. The heart of the forest was unlike anything he had ever experienced, a place where the magic of the land was tangible, pulsing just beneath the surface. It was both exhilarating and a little unnerving.

As they continued deeper into the forest, they came across more signs of the ancient magic that lay hidden here. They found a ring of stones, each one carved with intricate symbols that glowed faintly in the dim light. They discovered a tree with leaves that shimmered like gold, and when they touched it, they felt a warmth spread through their bodies, as if the tree was sharing its energy with them.

But as much as they were captivated by the beauty and magic of the forest, they couldn't forget the warning they had received. The heart of the forest was a place of power, and they needed to be cautious.

After walking for several hours, they reached a large clearing that took their breath away. In the center of the clearing was a massive tree, its trunk as wide as a small house and its branches stretching high into the sky. The tree's bark was a deep, rich brown, and its leaves shimmered with a silver light that seemed to pulse with a rhythm all its own.

Katie approached the tree cautiously, her eyes wide with wonder. "Jainu, look at this tree. It's incredible."

Jainu followed her, equally awed by the sight. The tree was ancient, its roots twisting and curling into the ground, and there was a sense of immense power emanating from it.

As they stood before the tree, Jainu noticed something strange. The symbols they had seen on the stones and the archway were carved into the tree's bark, glowing faintly in the dim light.

Katie reached out to touch the tree, her fingers brushing against the rough bark. As soon as her skin made contact, the symbols began to glow brighter, and the air around them seemed to hum with energy.

Jainu felt a shiver run down his spine as he watched the tree react to Katie's touch. There was something ancient and powerful about this place, something that made him feel both awed and a little afraid.

"Katie," he said quietly, his voice trembling slightly. "I think this tree is important. It's connected to the magic of the forest."

Katie nodded, her eyes never leaving the tree. "I think you're right, Jainu. There's something here, something we're meant to find."

As they stood before the tree, the air around them grew still, and the light from the symbols seemed to intensify. Jainu could feel the energy of the forest pulsing around them, as if the very ground beneath their feet was alive with magic.

Then, without warning, the ground began to tremble. The tree's branches swayed, and the symbols carved into its bark glowed with a brilliant light. Jainu and Katie stumbled back, watching in awe as the tree seemed to come to life.

A soft, melodic voice filled the air, echoing through the clearing. "Welcome, travelers," the voice said, its tone gentle and soothing. "You have entered the heart of the forest, the place where the magic of the land is strongest."

Jainu's eyes widened as he realized the voice was coming from the tree itself. The ancient tree was speaking to them, its words filled with wisdom and power.

"Who are you?" Katie asked, her voice filled with awe.

"I am the Guardian of the Forest," the tree replied. "I have watched over this land for countless ages, protecting its magic and guiding those who seek its power."

Jainu felt a deep sense of reverence as he listened to the Guardian's words. The tree was ancient, older than anything he had ever known, and its presence filled him with a sense of awe and respect.

"Why have you come here?" the Guardian asked, its voice soft but commanding.

Jainu hesitated for a moment before answering. "We're explorers. We were drawn to this place by the magic of the forest. We want to learn more about it, to understand its power."

The Guardian was silent for a moment, as if considering his words. "The magic of the forest is ancient and powerful," it said finally. "It is not to be taken lightly. Those who seek its power must be prepared to face great challenges."

Katie stepped forward, her eyes filled with determination. "We're ready," she said firmly. "We want to learn, to explore. We'll do whatever it takes."

The Guardian seemed to approve of her resolve, and the light from the symbols softened, becoming a gentle glow. "Very well," it said. "I will guide you, but you must be prepared for what lies ahead. The path you have chosen is not an easy one, and the magic of the forest is not always kind."

Jainu nodded, feeling a mixture of excitement and trepidation. The adventure they had embarked on was more than he had ever imagined, and he knew that the challenges ahead would test them in ways they couldn't yet foresee.

"What must we do?" Jainu asked, his voice steady.

"There is a great power hidden within the heart of the forest," the Guardian replied. "A power that has been locked away for centuries, waiting for those who are worthy to claim it. To find this power, you must follow the path that I will show you. But be warned—this path is fraught with danger, and not all who seek it will survive."

Katie and Jainu exchanged a glance, both of them understanding the gravity of the situation. This was no ordinary adventure—they were about to embark on a journey that could change their lives forever.

"We're ready," Katie said, her voice filled with determination. "Show us the way."

The Guardian's light intensified, and the ground beneath their feet began to glow with a soft, pulsing light. The symbols on the tree's bark seemed to shift and change, forming a new pattern that stretched out before them, leading deeper into the forest.

"Follow the path," the Guardian instructed. "It will lead you to the source of the forest's magic. But be cautious—the forest is alive, and it will test you. Only those who are pure of heart and strong of spirit will succeed."

Jainu felt a sense of resolve settle over him as he looked at the path that had been revealed. This was what they had been searching for, the reason they had been drawn to the heart of the forest. And now, with the Guardian's guidance, they were ready to face whatever challenges lay ahead.

"Thank you," Jainu said, his voice filled with gratitude. "We won't let you down."

The Guardian's light softened, and the tree's branches swayed gently in the breeze. "May the magic of the forest guide and protect you," it said, its voice fading as the light dimmed. "Good luck, travelers."

As the Guardian's voice faded into the background, Jainu and Katie stood in silence for a moment, both of them processing what had just happened. The path before them was illuminated by the soft glow of the symbols, and they knew that this was the beginning of a new and dangerous journey.

"Are you ready for this?" Jainu asked quietly, turning to Katie.

Katie nodded, her expression serious. "I'm ready. We've come this far, Jainu. We can't turn back now."

Jainu felt a surge of determination at her words. He knew that they were about to face incredible challenges, but with Katie by his side, he felt stronger, more capable of handling whatever came their way.

"Let's do this," he said, his voice filled with resolve.

Together, they stepped onto the path, the soft glow of the symbols lighting their way as they ventured deeper into the heart of the forest. The trees closed in around them, their branches forming a dense canopy that blocked out most of the sunlight. The air grew cooler, and the sounds of the forest seemed to fade, replaced by a heavy silence.

As they walked, Jainu couldn't shake the feeling that they were being watched. But it wasn't the same feeling of being observed by the forest—it was something else, something darker. The air felt thick with tension, and Jainu's senses were on high alert.

"Katie, do you feel that?" he asked quietly, his eyes scanning the trees around them.

Katie nodded, her expression tense. "Yeah, I do. Something's not right."

They continued on, their steps cautious and deliberate. The path seemed to wind endlessly through the forest, leading them deeper into the unknown. The trees grew taller and more twisted, their trunks covered in thick, dark moss. The air was heavy with the scent of damp earth and decaying leaves, and the ground beneath their feet was uneven and treacherous.

After what felt like hours, they came to a sudden stop. The path ahead was blocked by a thick wall of thorns, their sharp points glinting in the dim light. The thorns were woven tightly together, forming an impenetrable barrier that stretched as far as they could see.

Katie frowned, her eyes narrowing as she examined the barrier. "This must be one of the tests the Guardian warned us about."

Jainu nodded, his mind racing as he tried to think of a way to get past the thorns. "There has to be a way through. We just need to figure it out."

Katie reached out to touch the thorns, but as soon as her fingers made contact, the thorns seemed to come to life, twisting and writhing like snakes. She quickly pulled her hand back, her eyes wide with shock.

"Okay, that's definitely not normal," she muttered, shaking her head.

Jainu stepped forward, careful not to touch the thorns. He could feel the magic in the air, a dark and powerful energy that seemed to radiate from the barrier. The thorns were more than just a physical obstacle—they were alive, infused with the magic of the forest.

"There has to be a way to deactivate them," Jainu said, his voice thoughtful. "The Guardian wouldn't have sent us this way if there wasn't a way through."

Katie nodded in agreement. "Maybe there's a clue nearby. Something that will help us figure out how to get past this."

They began to search the area, carefully examining the ground and the trees around them. Jainu kept his eyes on the thorns, watching for any signs of movement. The dark energy in the air was oppressive, and he could feel it pressing down on him, making it hard to think clearly.

Then, out of the corner of his eye, Jainu spotted something—a small stone, half-buried in the ground. He knelt down and brushed away the dirt, revealing a symbol carved into the surface of the stone. It was the same symbol they had seen on the tree, glowing faintly in the dim light.

"Katie, look at this," Jainu said, holding up the stone for her to see.

Katie's eyes widened as she recognized the symbol. "That's it! That's the same symbol from the tree. Maybe it's the key to getting past the thorns."

Jainu nodded, feeling a surge of hope. The stone was small, but it seemed to pulse with energy, as if it was connected to the magic of the forest. He held it up to the barrier, watching as the thorns seemed to react to its presence, twitching and writhing in response.

"Maybe we need to use the stone to deactivate the thorns," Jainu suggested, holding the stone out in front of him.

Katie nodded, her eyes filled with determination. "It's worth a try. Let's do it."

Jainu stepped closer to the barrier, holding the stone in front of him as he approached. The thorns twisted and writhed, but they didn't lash out, as if they were waiting for something.

Taking a deep breath, Jainu placed the stone against the barrier, pressing it into the thick wall of thorns. As soon as the stone made contact, the symbols on its surface began to glow brightly, filling the clearing with a soft, pulsing light.

The thorns responded immediately, their movements becoming more frantic as the light intensified. Then, with a sudden burst of energy, the thorns began to unravel, pulling back and untwisting from each other. The wall of thorns dissolved before their eyes, revealing the path ahead.

Jainu and Katie exchanged a look of relief and triumph. They had passed the first test, and the way forward was clear.

"Nice work, Jainu," Katie said with a grin, clapping him on the shoulder.

Jainu smiled, feeling a sense of accomplishment. "Thanks. But I have a feeling this won't be the last challenge we face."

Katie nodded, her expression serious. "You're probably right. But we'll face whatever comes our way, together."

Jainu felt a warmth in his chest at her words. They were in this together, and as long as they had each other, he knew they could overcome any obstacle.

With the path now clear, they continued on, venturing deeper into the heart of the forest. The air was thick with tension, and they both knew that the challenges ahead would only get harder. But they were ready, determined to see their journey through to the end.

As they walked, Jainu couldn't shake the feeling that they were being watched. The presence he had felt earlier was still there, lurking just out of sight. But it wasn't the same dark energy that had surrounded the barrier of thorns—it was something else, something older and more powerful.

"Katie, do you feel that?" Jainu asked quietly, glancing around the dense forest.

Katie nodded, her expression tense. "Yeah, I do. It's like something's watching us, but I can't tell where it's coming from."

They continued on, their steps cautious and deliberate. The path seemed to wind endlessly through the forest, leading them deeper into the unknown. The trees grew taller and more twisted, their trunks covered in thick, dark moss. The air was heavy with the scent of damp earth and decaying leaves, and the ground beneath their feet was uneven and treacherous.

After what felt like hours, they came to a sudden stop. The path ahead opened up into a large clearing, and in the center stood a massive stone structure, ancient and weathered by time. The structure was covered in the same intricate symbols they had seen before, glowing faintly in the dim light.

Katie's eyes widened as she took in the sight. "Jainu, look at this. It's incredible."

Jainu nodded, equally awed by the sight. The structure was ancient, its stones worn smooth by the passage of time, but there was a sense of immense power emanating from it.

"This must be the next challenge," Jainu said quietly, his eyes scanning the structure.

Katie nodded in agreement. "We need to figure out what this is and how to get through it."

As they approached the structure, they noticed a series of large stones arranged in a circle around the base. Each stone was carved with the same symbols they had seen before, but these were larger and more elaborate.

Jainu reached out to touch one of the stones, feeling the rough texture beneath his fingers. As soon as he made contact, the symbols on the stone began to glow brighter, and the air around them seemed to hum with energy.

Katie watched in awe as the stones reacted to Jainu's touch. "It's like the stones are connected to the magic of the forest. Maybe they're the key to getting through this challenge."

Jainu nodded, his mind racing as he tried to figure out what to do next. The stones were clearly important, but he wasn't sure how they were supposed to use them.

Then, as if in response to his thoughts, the symbols on the stones began to shift and change, forming a new pattern that stretched out before them, leading up to the entrance of the structure.

Jainu and Katie exchanged a look of determination. This was the next step in their journey, and they were ready to face whatever challenges lay ahead.

"Let's do this," Jainu said, his voice steady.

Together, they stepped forward, following the path of symbols that led to the entrance of the structure. The air was thick with magic, and they could feel the energy of the forest pulsing around them, guiding them forward.

As they reached the entrance, the symbols on the stones flared with a bright light, illuminating the path ahead. Jainu and Katie took a deep breath and stepped inside, ready to face whatever awaited them in the heart of the forest.

Chapter 3

Trials of the Ancient Forest

The dense canopy of the ancient forest stretched above them, casting dappled shadows on the moss-covered ground below. The air was thick with the scent of pine, earth, and something else— something more profound that Jainu couldn't quite place. It was as if the forest itself breathed, its life force palpable in the very air around them.

Jainu and Katie moved cautiously, their senses heightened as they ventured deeper into the heart of the forest. The path before them, once a well-worn trail, had long since been overtaken by nature. Roots twisted and tangled across the ground, and the underbrush grew thick, making their progress slow and deliberate.

"There's something different about this place," Katie murmured, her voice barely above a whisper. Her eyes scanned the surrounding trees, their ancient trunks towering above them like silent sentinels.

Jainu nodded, feeling the same unease. "It's like the forest is watching us, testing us somehow."

The trees here were older than any they had seen before, their bark gnarled and twisted with age. The forest felt alive, its presence almost sentient, as if it were aware of their intrusion and was quietly assessing whether they were worthy of continuing further.

After hours of walking, they emerged into a small clearing, where the trees gave way to a circle of ancient stone pillars. The pillars were arranged in a perfect circle, each one carved with intricate symbols that glowed faintly in the dim light filtering through the canopy.

"This must be it," Katie said, her voice filled with awe as she approached the nearest pillar. "The center of the forest's magic."

Jainu followed her, his eyes scanning the carvings on the pillars. The symbols were unlike anything he had seen before, swirling patterns that seemed to shift and change when he wasn't looking directly at them. The air around the pillars was thick with energy, a low hum that reverberated through his bones.

At the center of the circle stood a massive stone altar, its surface etched with even more complex carvings. The altar seemed to pulse with a soft, inner light, as if it were alive with the very magic of the forest.

Katie reached out to touch one of the pillars, her fingers brushing against the cool stone. "It's warm," she said, surprised. "Like it's alive."

Jainu frowned, his senses on high alert. "Be careful. We don't know what kind of magic this is."

Katie nodded, pulling her hand back. "I know, but... it doesn't feel dangerous. It feels... welcoming."

Jainu studied the altar, his mind racing. "The Guardian mentioned a great power hidden within the forest. This must be it. But we need to be careful. The magic here is ancient, and who knows what kind of traps or challenges it might hold."

They circled the altar, examining the carvings for any clues that might help them unlock the secrets of the forest. The symbols were complex, shifting and changing as they watched, making it difficult to focus on any one detail.

"This is going to be tricky," Katie said, her brow furrowed in concentration as she tried to make sense of the symbols. "It's like the forest is hiding something from us, keeping its secrets just out of reach."

Jainu was silent for a moment, his mind racing as he studied the carvings. "Maybe we're approaching this the wrong way. Instead of trying to force the answers, maybe we need to let the magic guide us."

Katie looked at him, her eyes filled with curiosity. "What do you mean?"

Jainu took a deep breath, his hand hovering over the surface of the altar. "The magic here is alive, connected to the forest and everything in it. If we can tap into that connection, maybe the forest will reveal its secrets to us."

Katie nodded slowly, her expression thoughtful. "It's worth a try. But how do we tap into the magic?"

Jainu closed his eyes, focusing on the energy that pulsed around them. The air was thick with it, like a living presence that thrummed beneath the surface of the world. He could feel the magic coursing through the ground, through the trees, and even through his own body, as if he were a part of the forest itself.

Katie followed his lead, closing her eyes and reaching out with her senses. She could feel the magic too, a warm, comforting presence that seemed to wrap around her like a protective cloak. It was a strange feeling, both familiar and alien at the same time, as if she were tapping into something ancient and powerful that had existed long before she was born.

For a moment, they stood there in silence, their minds and bodies attuned to the magic of the forest. The air around them seemed to shimmer, the symbols on the altar glowing brighter as the connection between them and the forest deepened.

Then, without warning, the symbols on the altar flared with light, and the ground beneath their feet trembled. The air was filled with a low, resonant hum, like the sound of a thousand voices chanting in unison. The light from the altar spread out in ripples, like waves on a pond, and the stones around them began to glow with the same ethereal light.

Jainu and Katie opened their eyes, their hearts pounding in their chests as they took in the sight before them. The entire clearing was bathed in a soft, golden light, the trees around them glowing with an inner radiance that made the forest feel alive in a way it never had before.

The symbols on the altar shifted and changed, the swirling patterns rearranging themselves into a new configuration. The air was thick with magic, the power of the forest pulsing around them like a heartbeat.

"This is it," Jainu said, his voice filled with awe. "The key to the forest's magic."

Katie nodded, her eyes wide with wonder. "But what do we do with it? How do we use it?"

Jainu stared at the altar, his mind racing as he tried to make sense of the symbols. The patterns were complex, their meaning just out of reach, but there was something about them that felt familiar, as if he had seen them before in another time and place.

"We need to unlock the magic," Jainu said slowly, his eyes narrowing as he studied the carvings. "But we have to be careful. The magic here is powerful, and if we don't use it correctly, it could destroy us."

Katie looked at him, her expression serious. "What do you need me to do?"

Jainu took a deep breath, his mind focused on the task at hand. "We need to channel the magic, guide it in the right direction. I'll start the ritual, but I'll need your help to control the energy."

Katie nodded, her determination clear in her eyes. "I'm ready."

Jainu stepped closer to the altar, his hands hovering over the glowing symbols. He could feel the magic pulsing beneath his fingertips, like a living thing waiting to be unleashed. He began to chant softly, the words of the ancient language flowing from his lips like a river of power.

The symbols on the altar flared with light, and the air around them crackled with energy. Katie could feel the magic building, like a storm gathering on the horizon. She reached out with her mind, connecting with the energy, guiding it, shaping it into a form that they could control.

The air was filled with the sound of their chanting, the ancient words resonating with the magic of the forest. The light from the altar grew brighter, the symbols shifting and changing as the ritual progressed.

For a moment, it felt like they were on the verge of losing control, the magic slipping through their fingers like sand. But then, with a final burst of energy, the ritual was complete, and the light from the altar faded, leaving behind a soft, golden glow.

Jainu and Katie stood in silence, their breathing heavy as they took in the sight before them. The symbols on the altar had rearranged themselves into a new pattern, one that was clear and precise, like the solution to a puzzle that had been eluding them for years.

"This is it," Jainu said quietly, his voice filled with awe. "The key to unlocking the forest's magic."

Katie nodded, her eyes filled with wonder. "But what do we do with it?"

Jainu stared at the altar, his mind racing as he tried to make sense of the new pattern. The symbols were clear now, their meaning obvious, but there was something about them that still felt elusive, like a memory just out of reach.

"We need to take the key," Jainu said slowly, his hand hovering over the glowing symbols. "But we have to be careful. The magic here is powerful, and if we don't use it correctly, it could destroy us."

Katie reached out and placed her hand on Jainu's, her touch grounding him, calming the storm of thoughts in his mind. "We'll do it together," she said softly. "We can control the magic, guide it, just like we did before."

Jainu nodded, his resolve firming. "Together."

With a deep breath, they reached out and touched the key, their hands closing around the glowing crystal that had formed in the center of the altar. The moment they made contact, the air around them hummed with energy, and the ground beneath their feet trembled.

The forest responded to the release of the magic, the trees around them rustling as if in agreement. The light from the key spread out in a wave, flowing through the forest like a river, connecting everything in its path.

Jainu and Katie could feel the magic flowing through them, filling them with a sense of power and purpose. They were no longer just two people wandering through the forest—they were a part of it, connected to its magic in a way that they had never been before.

For a moment, the world around them seemed to blur, the lines between reality and magic fading as they became one with the forest. They could see the ancient guardians, the spirits of the forest, watching over them, their presence a comforting weight on their shoulders.

Then, as quickly as it had begun, the magic receded, leaving behind a sense of peace and calm. The key in their hands glowed softly, its light a reminder of the power they now held.

"We did it," Katie whispered, her voice filled with wonder. "We unlocked the magic of the forest."

Jainu nodded, his heart pounding with a mixture of excitement and awe. "But this is just the beginning. There's so much more to discover, so much more to learn."

Katie looked at him, her eyes filled with determination. "Then let's keep going. Let's find out what the forest has in store for us."

They left the altar and continued their journey through the forest, the key in hand guiding their way. The path ahead was long and winding, but they were no longer afraid. The forest was alive with magic, and they were a part of it, connected to its ancient power in a way that few people ever would be.

As they ventured further into the depths of the forest, the atmosphere around them grew more intense. The air seemed to hum with anticipation, and the dense foliage pressed in on them from all sides. The key they had retrieved from the altar glowed faintly, a constant reminder of the power they now held.

Katie held the key firmly in her hand, its warmth seeping into her skin. "This thing is amazing," she said, her voice filled with awe. "It's like it's alive, guiding us."

Jainu nodded, his gaze focused on the path ahead. "The magic here is unlike anything I've ever felt. It's almost as if the forest itself is communicating with us, showing us where to go."

They walked in silence for a while, the only sounds being the crunch of leaves underfoot and the distant calls of unseen creatures. The forest was a living, breathing entity, and they were now deeply entwined with its magic.

As they continued, the landscape around them began to change. The towering trees gave way to an area filled with massive, ancient oaks, their branches stretching out like the arms of giants. The ground was covered in thick, soft moss that muffled their footsteps, and the air was filled with the sweet scent of blooming flowers.

But something about this place felt different. The energy in the air was stronger, more concentrated, and it made the hairs on the back of Jainu's neck stand on end.

Katie stopped suddenly, her eyes widening. "Do you feel that?"

Jainu paused, turning to her. "What is it?"

"It's like… something's watching us." She glanced around nervously, her grip tightening on the key.

Jainu closed his eyes, reaching out with his senses. He could feel it too—a presence lurking just beyond the edge of his perception. It was subtle, almost imperceptible, but it was there, watching them, waiting.

"We're not alone," Jainu said quietly, his voice tense. "Something is here with us."

They stood still, listening intently to the sounds of the forest. For a moment, everything was silent, and then they heard it—a low, guttural growl coming from the shadows between the trees.

Jainu and Katie exchanged a glance, their hearts pounding in their chests. They knew that whatever was out there, it wasn't friendly.

Slowly, they began to back away, their eyes scanning the forest for any sign of movement. The growling grew louder, and then, with a sudden burst of speed, a massive creature leaped out of the shadows, its fangs bared and its eyes glowing with a malevolent light.

Jainu reacted instinctively, raising his hand to unleash a burst of magic at the creature. The force of the blast sent the creature flying back into the trees, but it quickly recovered, snarling as it prepared to attack again.

Katie held up the key, its light flaring brightly as she channeled its power. The creature hesitated, its eyes narrowing as it focused on the glowing object in her hand.

"Stay back!" Katie shouted, her voice firm.

The creature snarled, its eyes locked on the key. It was clear that the key was what it wanted, and it wasn't going to back down easily.

Jainu stepped forward, his hand glowing with magical energy. "You're not getting past us," he said, his voice filled with determination.

The creature growled, its muscles tensing as it prepared to pounce. But before it could make its move, the ground beneath it suddenly shifted, vines erupting from the earth and wrapping around its legs, pinning it in place.

Jainu and Katie watched in surprise as the creature struggled against the vines, but it was no use. The forest had come to their aid, its magic responding to their need.

"Let's get out of here," Katie said urgently, pulling Jainu away from the struggling creature.

They turned and ran, the key's light guiding them through the forest. Behind them, the creature roared in frustration, but it was unable to break free from the vines that held it.

They didn't stop running until they were well beyond the reach of the creature. Finally, they slowed to a stop, their breaths coming in ragged gasps as they leaned against a tree.

"That was close," Katie said, her voice shaky.

Jainu nodded, his heart still pounding. "Too close. But the forest… it helped us. It's like it knew we were in danger."

Katie looked down at the key in her hand, its light pulsing gently. "I think the key is connected to the forest somehow. It's like it's guiding us, protecting us."

Jainu frowned, his mind racing. "But why? What's so important about this key that the forest would protect us like that?"

Katie shook her head. "I don't know. But whatever it is, it must be incredibly powerful."

They stood in silence for a moment, each lost in their own thoughts. The encounter with the creature had shaken them, but it had also made them more determined than ever to uncover the secrets of the forest.

"We need to keep moving," Jainu said finally, his voice resolute. "There's still so much we don't know, and we can't stop now."

Katie nodded in agreement. "You're right. Let's keep going. The answers have to be out there somewhere."

They continued their journey, the forest around them growing darker and more foreboding as they pressed on. The trees were thicker here, their branches twisted and gnarled, and the underbrush was so dense that it was difficult to see the path ahead.

But they didn't waver. With the key's light guiding their way, they pushed forward, determined to uncover the truth that lay hidden within the heart of the forest.

As they walked, they began to notice more signs of the forest's ancient magic. Strange symbols were carved into the trunks of the trees, their meaning lost to time. The air was filled with a low, resonant hum, like the sound of a distant drumbeat that reverberated through their bones.

Jainu paused to examine one of the symbols, his hand tracing the lines carved into the bark. "These symbols... they're the same as the ones on the altar."

Katie looked at the symbol, her brow furrowed in concentration. "What do you think they mean?"

"I'm not sure," Jainu admitted. "But they're definitely connected to the magic of the forest. Maybe they're a way to channel the magic, or maybe they're a warning."

Katie glanced around nervously. "A warning of what?"

Jainu shook his head. "I don't know. But we need to be careful. The deeper we go, the more dangerous this place becomes."

They continued on, the forest around them growing darker and more oppressive with each step. The air was thick with tension, and the low hum in the background grew louder, like the beat of a war drum.

As they ventured deeper, the path became more treacherous. The ground was uneven, the roots of the ancient trees creating natural obstacles that tripped them up as they walked. The underbrush grew thicker, and the branches above them seemed to close in, blocking out the light.

"We're getting close to something," Katie said, her voice filled with a mix of anticipation and dread. "I can feel it."

Jainu nodded, his senses on high alert. "Me too. Whatever it is, it's powerful."

They pressed on, their footsteps cautious as they navigated the uneven terrain. The key in Katie's hand glowed brighter, its light cutting through the darkness like a beacon.

Suddenly, the path ahead opened up into a large clearing, and they found themselves standing at the edge of a massive chasm. The ground fell away into a deep abyss, the bottom lost in shadow. A narrow stone bridge spanned the chasm, its surface worn smooth by time.

On the other side of the bridge, a massive stone structure loomed, its walls covered in the same strange symbols they had seen throughout the forest. The structure was ancient, its edges softened by centuries of exposure to the elements, but it was clear that it had once been a place of great power.

"This is it," Jainu said, his voice filled with awe. "The heart of the forest's magic."

Katie stared at the structure, her heart pounding. "But how do we get across?"

Jainu stepped closer to the edge of the chasm, his eyes scanning the narrow bridge. "We'll have to cross the bridge. It's the only way."

Katie looked at the bridge nervously. It was narrow, barely wide enough for one person to walk across, and the drop below was dizzying. "It doesn't look safe."

Jainu nodded. "It's not. But we don't have a choice. We have to cross."

Katie swallowed hard, her hands trembling slightly. "Okay. Let's do it."

Jainu took the lead, stepping onto the bridge with a steadying breath. The stone was cold underfoot, and the wind howled through the chasm, making the bridge sway slightly. He moved cautiously, his eyes focused on the other side, each step deliberate and measured.

Katie followed close behind, her heart racing as she placed one foot in front of the other. The wind tugged at her clothes, threatening to throw her off balance, but she kept her gaze fixed on Jainu's back, willing herself to stay calm.

Halfway across the bridge, the wind picked up, growing stronger and more forceful. The bridge swayed dangerously, and Katie let out a small cry as she nearly lost her footing.

"Hang on!" Jainu shouted over the roar of the wind. He reached back, grabbing Katie's hand to steady her. "We're almost there!"

They pressed on, the wind buffeting them from all sides as they inched their way across the bridge. Finally, after what felt like an eternity, they reached the other side, their feet touching solid ground once more.

Katie let out a breath she hadn't realized she'd been holding, her legs trembling with relief. "That was… intense."

Jainu nodded, his expression grim. "The forest isn't making this easy for us. But we're not turning back now."

They turned to face the stone structure that loomed before them. It was massive, its walls rising high into the sky, and the symbols carved into its surface seemed to pulse with a faint, eerie light.

"This place… it's incredible," Katie whispered, her voice filled with awe as she took in the sight before her.

Jainu approached the entrance cautiously, his senses on high alert. "It's more than that. It's powerful. The magic here is unlike anything we've encountered before."

The entrance to the structure was a massive stone door, its surface covered in the same intricate symbols. The door was sealed shut, and there was no visible handle or keyhole.

"This must be the entrance," Katie said, her voice tinged with excitement. "But how do we open it?"

Jainu examined the door closely, his hand tracing the symbols carved into the stone. "There has to be a way. Maybe the key can unlock it."

Katie nodded, holding up the key. "Let's try it."

She placed the key against the door, its light flaring brightly as it made contact with the stone. The symbols on the door glowed in response, their light spreading out in ripples across the surface.

For a moment, nothing happened. Then, with a low rumble, the stone door slowly began to slide open, revealing a dark, narrow corridor beyond.

Jainu and Katie exchanged a look of triumph. They had succeeded—the door was open, and the way forward was clear.

"Nice work, Katie," Jainu said with a grin, clapping her on the shoulder.

Katie smiled, her heart swelling with pride. "Thanks. But this is just the beginning."

They stepped into the corridor, the soft glow of the key illuminating the path ahead. The air inside was cool, almost cold, and it carried with it a faint, musty scent, as if the place had been sealed off from the outside world for centuries.

The walls of the corridor were lined with more carvings, the same swirling patterns they had seen throughout the forest. The symbols seemed to pulse with a faint, inner light, casting eerie shadows on the stone floor.

"This place feels… different," Katie said, her voice barely above a whisper as they moved deeper into the structure. "Like we're walking through history."

Jainu nodded, his eyes scanning the carvings on the walls. "These symbols… they're telling a story. I think it's the history of the forest, of how it came to be."

They continued down the corridor, their footsteps echoing softly in the silence. The deeper they ventured, the stronger the sense of power became, as if they were approaching the very core of the forest's magic.

As they reached the end of the corridor, they found themselves standing before another massive stone door. This one was even larger than the first, its surface covered in intricate carvings that glowed with a soft, golden light.

"This must be the final chamber," Jainu said, his voice filled with anticipation. "The heart of the forest's magic."

Katie stared at the door, her heart pounding. "But how do we open it?"

Jainu held up the key, its light pulsing gently. "I think the key will unlock it, just like before."

He placed the key against the door, its light flaring brightly as it made contact with the stone. The symbols on the door glowed in response, their light spreading out in ripples across the surface.

With a low rumble, the stone door slowly began to slide open, revealing a large, circular chamber beyond. The chamber was vast, its ceiling lost in shadow, and the walls were lined with ancient stone columns.

In the center of the chamber stood a massive stone altar, similar to the one they had seen before, but this one was different. The altar was covered in intricate carvings, the symbols glowing with a soft, golden light.

"This is it," Jainu said quietly, his voice filled with awe. "The heart of the forest's magic."

Katie nodded, her eyes wide with wonder. "But what do we do now?"

Jainu stepped closer to the altar, his eyes scanning the symbols. "We need to unlock the magic, just like before."

Katie followed him, her heart pounding with anticipation. "But how do we do that?"

Jainu held up the key, its light pulsing gently. "I think the key is the answer. It's connected to the forest's magic, and if we use it correctly, we can unlock the power that's been hidden here for centuries."

Katie stared at the key, her mind racing with possibilities. "But what if we make a mistake? What if we unlock something we can't control?"

Jainu met her gaze, his expression serious. "We have to be careful. But we've come this far, and we can't turn back now. We need to see this through to the end."

Katie nodded, her resolve firming. "You're right. Let's do this."

With a deep breath, they approached the altar, the key in hand guiding their way. The air around them was thick with magic, the power of the forest pulsing through the chamber like a living presence.

Jainu placed the key on the altar, its light flaring brightly as it made contact with the stone. The symbols on the altar glowed in response, their light spreading out in ripples across the surface.

For a moment, nothing happened. Then, with a sudden burst of energy, the altar flared with light, and the air around them was filled with a blinding brilliance. Jainu and Katie felt a surge of power course through them, as if the magic of the forest was flowing into their very beings.

Katie gasped, her eyes widening as the magic filled her. It was a strange, exhilarating feeling, like she was being lifted off the ground, weightless and free.

Jainu felt the magic too, a powerful force that seemed to resonate with the very core of his being.

It was like nothing he had ever experienced before, a connection to the forest and its ancient magic that went beyond words.

As the light began to fade, Jainu and Katie opened their eyes, their hearts still pounding with the intensity of the experience. The key in their hands was now cool, its light dimmed, but the connection they felt with the forest remained strong.

"We did it," Katie whispered, her voice filled with wonder. "We unlocked the magic of the forest."

Jainu nodded, his heart pounding with a mixture of excitement and awe. "But this is just the beginning. There's so much more to discover, so much more to learn."

Katie looked at him, her eyes filled with determination. "Then let's keep going. Let's find out what the forest has in store for us."

They turned and left the chamber, the key in hand guiding their way. The path ahead was long and winding, but they were no longer afraid. The forest was alive with magic, and they were a part of it, connected to its ancient power in a way that few people ever would be.

As they walked, they could feel the forest responding to their presence, the trees swaying gently in the breeze, the animals watching them from the shadows. It was as if the forest itself was guiding them, showing them the way forward.

They came across more ancient stone pillars, each one covered in the same intricate carvings they had seen before. The symbols on the pillars glowed faintly, their light guiding them through the dense underbrush.

"This forest is incredible," Katie said, her voice filled with awe as she took in the sights around them. "It's like it's alive, like it's watching over us."

Jainu nodded, his eyes scanning the trees around them. "It is alive. The magic here... it's connected to everything in the forest. We're just a part of it, a small piece of a much larger puzzle."

They continued walking, the path beneath their feet becoming more defined as they ventured deeper into the forest. The air was thick with magic, the power of the forest pulsing around them like a living presence.

After several hours of walking, they came across a small stream, its water crystal clear and shimmering with a soft, golden light. The stream's banks were lined with flowers, their petals glowing in the sunlight, and the air was filled with the gentle sound of the water flowing over the rocks.

Jainu and Katie knelt by the stream, their hands cupped to drink the cool, refreshing water. As they drank, they felt the magic of the forest flowing through them, filling them with a sense of peace and renewal.

"This water... it's like nothing I've ever tasted before," Katie said, her voice filled with wonder. "It's like it's alive, filled with the magic of the forest."

Jainu nodded, feeling the same sense of awe. "It is. This whole forest... it's alive, filled with magic. And we're a part of it now."

They continued on, following the stream as it wound its way through the forest. The path was lined with more flowers, their petals glowing in the sunlight, and the air was filled with the scent of blooming blossoms.

As they walked, they noticed more signs of the forest's magic. They came across a grove of trees, their trunks twisted and gnarled, their branches intertwined to form a dense canopy overhead. The light filtering through the leaves cast a soft, golden glow over the grove, and the air was filled with the scent of pine and earth.

In the center of the grove stood a small stone altar, similar to the ones they had seen before, but this one was different. The altar was covered in intricate carvings, the symbols glowing faintly in the dim light. The air around the altar was thick with magic, and Jainu and Katie could feel its power resonating in the air around them.

They approached the altar cautiously, their steps slow and reverent. The magic here was strong, more powerful than anything they had felt before, and they knew that they were standing in a place of great significance.

"This altar... it feels different from the others," Katie said, her voice hushed. "The magic here is stronger, more intense."

Jainu nodded, feeling the same sense of awe. "It's like the forest is guiding us here, showing us something important."

As they stood before the altar, the symbols began to glow brighter, their light spreading out in ripples across the surface of the stone. The air around them hummed with energy, and Jainu could feel the magic of the forest resonating with the altar, unlocking the ancient power that lay within.

For a moment, they stood in silence, the light from the symbols surrounding them, the magic of the altar flowing through them. It was a moment of pure connection, of unity with the forest and its ancient power.

Then, as the light began to fade, Jainu and Katie opened their eyes, their hearts still filled with the warmth of the magic. The crystal in Jainu's hand was now cool, its light dimmed, but the connection they felt with the forest remained strong.

"Do you think the magic will guide us to where we need to go next?" Katie asked, her voice filled with wonder.

Jainu nodded, his gaze still on the altar. "I believe so. This forest... it's more than just a place. It's like a living entity, and it wants to protect its secrets. But now that we've unlocked this part of its magic, I think it will guide us to the next step."

Katie smiled, her heart swelling with the possibilities of what lay ahead. "I can't wait to see what comes next."

As they left the grove and continued their journey, they felt a renewed sense of purpose. The forest was alive with magic, and they were connected to it in a way that few had ever been. The path before them was long and filled with unknown challenges, but they knew they would face whatever came their way together.

Chapter 4

The Entrance to the Enchanted Labyrinth

The forest seemed to stretch endlessly around Jainu and Katie as they ventured deeper into its heart. The air grew cooler, and the towering trees closed in on them, their thick branches intertwining above like the arches of a cathedral. The ground beneath their feet was soft with moss, and the scent of pine needles and damp earth filled their nostrils. Each step seemed to take them further from the world they knew and deeper into one ruled by ancient magic.

"It feels like the forest is swallowing us," Katie murmured, her voice barely audible over the rustle of leaves. Her eyes darted around nervously, searching the shadows between the trees for any sign of movement.

Jainu nodded, his expression grim. "It's like the forest is alive, guiding us—or maybe trying to trap us."

They had been following a faint trail that wound through the dense underbrush, but the path had become increasingly difficult to discern. The forest seemed to change around them, as if the trees were shifting positions, altering the landscape to confuse them. More than once, they had doubled back, only to find themselves standing at the same spot they had left minutes earlier.

Katie frowned, glancing up at the dark canopy overhead. "I feel like we're walking in circles. How do we know we're even going the right way?"

Jainu reached into his pocket and pulled out the crystal key they had retrieved earlier. The key glowed faintly in his hand, its light pulsing in rhythm with the beat of his heart. "This is guiding us," he said, holding it up for her to see. "As long as we have this, we'll find our way."

Katie sighed, nodding. "I hope you're right. This place is giving me the creeps."

They pressed on, the silence between them filled with the sounds of the forest. The further they walked, the more the path seemed to narrow, until they were forced to push through thick underbrush and duck under low-hanging branches. The trees grew taller and more twisted, their roots protruding from the ground like the fingers of a giant hand.

Then, suddenly, the trees parted, and they found themselves standing in a small clearing. In the center of the clearing was an ancient stone archway, its surface covered in intricate carvings that seemed to shimmer in the dim light. The archway was massive, towering over them, and it emitted a low, steady hum that resonated in their bones.

Katie approached the archway cautiously, her hand outstretched. "This must be it," she whispered, her voice filled with awe. "The entrance to the labyrinth."

Jainu nodded, his eyes fixed on the archway. "It has to be. The Guardian mentioned a labyrinth—a place where the ancient magic of the forest is strongest. This must be the way in."

Katie's fingers brushed against the cool stone of the archway, and as they did, the carvings flared with light, casting the clearing in a soft, golden glow. A gentle breeze swept through the trees, rustling the leaves and sending a shiver down her spine.

Jainu stepped forward, his hand resting on the hilt of his sword as he scanned the clearing for any signs of danger. "Be careful," he warned. "We don't know what's waiting for us inside."

Katie nodded, pulling her hand back. "I know. But we've come this far—we can't turn back now."

Taking a deep breath, they stepped through the archway together. The moment they crossed the threshold, the world around them seemed to shift. The air grew heavier, and a palpable sense of magic enveloped them, as if they had entered a different realm entirely. The light dimmed, and the vibrant colors of the forest faded into muted shades of gray and green.

They found themselves standing in a narrow corridor, its walls lined with the same intricate carvings they had seen on the archway. The floor was smooth and cold underfoot, and the air was filled with a low, constant hum that seemed to echo from the very stones themselves.

"This place… it's like we've stepped into another world," Katie whispered, her voice filled with awe as she gazed at the carvings on the walls.

Jainu nodded, his eyes scanning the corridor. "It feels ancient—like it's been here for centuries, hidden away from the rest of the world."

The First Challenge

They began to move cautiously down the corridor, their footsteps echoing softly off the stone walls. The carvings grew more elaborate as they continued, depicting scenes of ancient battles, rituals, and figures shrouded in mystery. The hum grew louder, vibrating through the stone and into their bones, a constant reminder of the power that lay hidden within the labyrinth.

As they rounded a corner, they found themselves standing at the entrance to a vast chamber. The ceiling was so high that it disappeared into shadow, and the walls were lined with towering stone columns. In the center of the chamber stood a massive stone pedestal, its surface covered in glowing symbols.

"This must be the heart of the labyrinth," Katie said, her voice filled with awe as she approached the pedestal. "The place where the ancient magic is strongest."

Jainu followed her, his eyes fixed on the pedestal. "It has to be. But we need to be careful—there's no telling what kind of traps or challenges might be waiting for us here."

Katie reached out to touch the pedestal, but before her fingers could make contact, the ground beneath them began to tremble. The symbols on the pedestal flared with light, and a low rumble echoed through the chamber.

They jumped back as the pedestal split down the middle, revealing a hidden compartment within. Inside the compartment was a small, glowing orb, its surface swirling with a strange, ethereal light.

"What is that?" Katie asked, her eyes wide as she stared at the orb.

Jainu hesitated, his instincts warning him to be cautious. "I'm not sure… but it's definitely powerful."

Katie reached out to pick up the orb, but as soon as her fingers brushed against it, the chamber around them began to change. The columns shifted and moved, rearranging themselves into a complex maze of stone walls and narrow passageways.

Jainu and Katie found themselves standing at the entrance to the newly formed maze, the glowing orb hovering between them. The hum of the magic grew louder, filling the air with a sense of urgency.

"It's a challenge," Jainu said, his voice tense. "The labyrinth is testing us."

Katie looked around, her heart racing. "We have to find our way through this maze… but how?"

Jainu stared at the orb, its light reflecting in his eyes. "Maybe the orb can guide us. It's connected to the magic here—if we follow it, we might be able to find our way out."

He reached out and took the orb in his hand. The moment he did, the orb flared with light, illuminating the maze around them. The walls seemed to pulse in time with the light, creating a path that led deeper into the labyrinth.

"Let's go," Jainu said, his voice filled with determination.

They entered the maze, the orb lighting their way as they navigated the twisting corridors and narrow passageways. The walls of the maze were smooth and cold, and the air was filled with the scent of ancient stone and dust. The maze seemed to stretch on forever, each turn leading them deeper into the heart of the labyrinth.

The Maze of Memories

As they ventured further into the maze, they began to notice something strange. The walls of the maze were no longer bare stone—instead, they were covered in intricate carvings that depicted scenes from their own lives. The images were so detailed that it was as if they were walking through a living memory.

Katie stopped in front of one of the carvings, her eyes widening in shock. "Jainu... look at this."

Jainu turned to see what she was looking at. The carving depicted a young Katie, standing in a sunlit meadow, her arms outstretched as she called out to someone in the distance. The details were so vivid that Jainu could almost hear the sound of her voice, the warmth of the sun on her skin.

"This... this is from when I was a child," Katie said, her voice trembling with emotion. "I used to play in that meadow every day... how could the labyrinth know this?"

Jainu reached out to touch the carving, but as soon as his fingers brushed against the stone, the image changed. The meadow faded, replaced by a scene from Jainu's past—a memory of him standing alone on a snowy mountaintop, the wind howling around him as he stared out at the distant horizon.

"This is… incredible," Jainu whispered, his voice filled with awe. "The labyrinth is showing us our own memories… but why?"

Katie shook her head, her mind racing. "I don't know… maybe it's trying to remind us of something, or maybe it's trying to test us."

They continued through the maze, the walls around them shifting and changing as they moved. Each turn brought new memories to life—moments of joy and sorrow, triumph and defeat. The labyrinth seemed to be drawing out their deepest emotions, forcing them to confront their pasts as they navigated its twisting corridors.

As they walked, Jainu couldn't help but feel a sense of unease. The memories were so vivid, so real, that it was as if they were living through them all over again. But there was something more—something lurking just beneath the surface of their memories, waiting to be uncovered.

Katie stopped suddenly, her breath catching in her throat as she stared at the wall in front of her. The carving depicted a scene she had tried to forget—a moment of pain and regret that she had buried deep within her heart.

"Jainu… I can't do this," she whispered, her voice trembling with emotion. "I can't face this memory… it's too painful."

Jainu placed a comforting hand on her shoulder, his voice gentle. "You don't have to face it alone. I'm here with you."

Katie nodded, tears welling up in her eyes as she stared at the carving. The memory was too vivid, too real—it was as if she was reliving that moment all over again. But with Jainu by her side, she found the strength to confront it.

"This memory… it's from when I lost someone I cared about," Katie said, her voice choked with emotion. "I was so young… I didn't know how to handle the pain. I tried to forget, but the memory has haunted me ever since."

Jainu squeezed her shoulder, his voice filled with understanding. "We all have memories like that, Katie. Moments of pain and regret that we try to bury, but they never really go away. The labyrinth is forcing us to confront those memories, to face our pasts so that we can move forward."

Katie nodded, wiping away her tears. "You're right... I need to face this. I need to let go of the past so that I can move on."

They continued through the maze, each step taking them deeper into their own memories. The labyrinth seemed to be testing them, forcing them to confront their deepest fears and regrets. But with each memory they faced, they grew stronger, more determined to find their way through the maze.

Finally, after what felt like hours of walking, they reached the center of the maze. In the middle of the chamber was a small, glowing crystal, its light pulsing gently. The walls around them were covered in intricate carvings, each one depicting a different memory from their past.

"This is it," Jainu said, his voice filled with awe. "The heart of the maze."

Katie stared at the crystal, her heart pounding with anticipation. "But what do we do now?"

Jainu reached out to touch the crystal, but before he could make contact, the air around them shimmered, and the walls of the maze began to shift and change. The carvings faded, replaced by a new scene—one that was all too familiar.

They found themselves standing in the middle of a battlefield, the air thick with the scent of smoke and blood. The sound of clashing swords and the cries of the wounded filled the air, and the ground beneath their feet was littered with the bodies of fallen soldiers.

"This… this is a memory from the war," Jainu whispered, his voice filled with shock. "But how… how is this possible?"

Katie's eyes widened in fear as she looked around at the carnage. "Jainu… we're not just seeing this memory… we're living it."

The battlefield stretched out before them, a chaotic scene of violence and death. Jainu could feel the weight of his sword in his hand, the heat of the sun on his back. The memory was so vivid, so real, that it was as if they had been transported back in time.

"We need to find a way out of here," Jainu said, his voice filled with urgency. "The labyrinth is testing us—it's trying to see if we can survive our own memories."

They began to move cautiously through the battlefield, their senses on high alert. The memory was so real that it was almost overwhelming—Jainu could feel the adrenaline pumping through his veins, the fear and determination that had driven him during the war.

But this was no ordinary memory. The labyrinth had twisted it, making the enemies they faced more powerful, more dangerous. The soldiers they fought were relentless, their attacks fueled by the dark magic of the labyrinth.

Katie fought bravely by Jainu's side, her movements swift and precise as she cut down enemy after enemy. But the battle seemed never-ending, the enemies coming at them in waves, each one more powerful than the last.

"We can't keep this up," Katie panted, her breath coming in ragged gasps. "We need to find a way to end this."

Jainu's mind raced as he tried to think of a solution. The labyrinth was feeding off their fear, using their memories against them. But there had to be a way to turn the tide, to take control of the memory and bend it to their will.

As they fought, Jainu began to notice something strange. The enemies they were facing were not just random soldiers—they were figures from his past, people he had known and fought alongside during the war. But there was something different about them, something twisted and wrong.

"These aren't just memories," Jainu realized, his voice filled with shock. "The labyrinth is twisting them, turning our past against us."

Katie's eyes widened in fear as she recognized one of the figures they were fighting. "Jainu… that's… that's my brother."

Jainu's heart sank as he realized what the labyrinth was doing. It was forcing them to confront their deepest fears and regrets, using the people they had loved and lost to break them.

But Jainu refused to let the labyrinth win. He gritted his teeth, focusing all his willpower on taking control of the memory. He could feel the magic of the labyrinth pulsing around him, trying to bend his mind to its will, but he fought back with everything he had.

"This is our memory," Jainu shouted, his voice filled with determination. "We control it—not the labyrinth!"

Katie nodded, her eyes filled with resolve. Together, they focused their willpower on taking control of the memory, forcing the twisted figures of their past to retreat. The battlefield around them began to change, the enemies fading into the shadows as they reclaimed their memories.

Finally, the battlefield disappeared, replaced by the calm, glowing chamber they had been in before. The crystal in the center of the chamber pulsed gently, its light a reminder of the power they now held.

"We did it," Katie whispered, her voice filled with awe. "We took control of the memory."

Jainu nodded, his heart pounding with a mixture of relief and pride. "But we're not done yet. The labyrinth is testing us—there's still more to come."

They approached the crystal cautiously, their senses on high alert. The air around them was thick with magic, the power of the labyrinth pulsing through the chamber like a living presence.

Jainu reached out to touch the crystal, and as soon as his fingers made contact, the air around them shimmered, and they were transported to another memory—one that was even more intense than the last.

The Trial of Courage

They found themselves standing on the edge of a cliff, the wind howling around them as the sea crashed against the rocks below. The sky was dark and stormy, and the air was filled with the scent of salt and rain.

"This is… this is where I faced my greatest fear," Katie whispered, her voice trembling with emotion. "This is where I almost lost everything."

Jainu stared at the scene before them, his heart pounding. The memory was so vivid that he could almost feel the cold wind on his skin, the spray of the ocean on his face. But there was something different about it—something more powerful, more dangerous.

"This isn't just a memory," Jainu realized, his voice filled with dread. "The labyrinth is amplifying it, making it more intense. We're going to have to face this fear all over again—but this time, it's going to be even harder."

Katie nodded, her expression filled with determination. "I'm ready. I've faced this fear before—I can do it again."

They began to make their way down the cliff, the wind and rain battering them from all sides. The path was narrow and treacherous, the rocks slick with seawater, and the drop below was dizzying.

As they descended, the memory began to shift and change. The wind grew stronger, the rain more intense, until it felt like they were walking through a hurricane. The path became narrower, the rocks more unstable, and the drop below seemed to stretch on forever.

But Katie refused to give up. She focused all her willpower on overcoming the fear that had gripped her during this memory, forcing herself to keep moving forward, one step at a time.

Jainu followed close behind, his eyes fixed on the path ahead. He could feel the magic of the labyrinth trying to break them, trying to push them over the edge, but he fought back with everything he had.

Finally, they reached the bottom of the cliff, the storm around them fading as they stepped onto solid ground. The memory began to dissolve, replaced by the glowing chamber they had been in before.

Katie let out a breath she hadn't realized she'd been holding, her legs trembling with relief. "We did it... we overcame the fear."

Jainu nodded, his heart filled with pride. "But the labyrinth isn't done with us yet. There's still more to come."

The Trial of the Heart

The next memory was one that neither of them had expected. They found themselves standing in a sunlit garden, the air filled with the scent of blooming flowers and the sound of birds singing. The sky was a brilliant shade of blue, and the sun shone down warmly on their faces.

"This is… this is where we first met," Katie whispered, her voice filled with wonder.

Jainu stared at the scene before them, his heart pounding with emotion. The memory was so vivid that it was as if they had been transported back to that very moment, to the day when their paths had first crossed.

"This is… beautiful," Jainu said, his voice filled with awe. "But why is the labyrinth showing us this?"

Katie shook her head, her mind racing. "I don't know… maybe it's trying to remind us of something. Something important."

They began to walk through the garden, the memory playing out around them like a living dream. They could see themselves as they had been on that day—two strangers brought together by fate, their lives intertwined by the magic of the forest.

As they walked, the memory began to shift and change, showing them moments from their journey together—moments of laughter and joy, of sorrow and pain. The labyrinth was reminding them of the bond they shared, of the love that had grown between them as they faced the trials of the forest together.

"This is… incredible," Katie whispered, her voice filled with emotion. "The labyrinth is showing us our journey—our story."

Jainu nodded, his eyes filled with tears. "It's reminding us of why we're here—of what we're fighting for."

As they continued through the garden, the memory began to fade, replaced by the glowing chamber they had been in before. The crystal in the center of the chamber pulsed gently, its light a reminder of the power they now held.

"We've faced our fears, our regrets, and our love," Katie said, her voice filled with determination. "But what's next? What more does the labyrinth want from us?"

Jainu stared at the crystal, his mind racing. "I don't know... but whatever it is, we'll face it together."

The Final Trial

The air around them shimmered, and they were transported to a new memory—one that was darker, more intense than anything they had faced before.

They found themselves standing in a dark forest, the trees towering above them like shadowy giants. The air was thick with the scent of decay, and the ground beneath their feet was soft and damp with rot.

"This is... this is where I lost my way," Jainu whispered, his voice filled with dread. "This is where I almost gave up."

Katie's eyes widened in fear as she looked around at the dark forest. "Jainu... we're not just seeing this memory... we're living it."

The forest around them was alive with dark magic, the shadows shifting and moving as if they were alive. The air was filled with a low, menacing hum, and the trees seemed to close in around them, trapping them in a world of darkness and despair.

"We need to find a way out of here," Jainu said, his voice filled with urgency. "The labyrinth is testing us—it's trying to see if we can overcome the darkness within ourselves."

They began to move cautiously through the forest, their senses on high alert. The memory was so real that it was almost overwhelming—Jainu could feel the fear and despair that had gripped him during this moment, the sense of hopelessness that had almost consumed him.

But this was no ordinary memory. The labyrinth had twisted it, amplifying the darkness and making it more powerful, more dangerous. The shadows around them were filled with unseen threats, and the air was thick with the scent of death and decay.

Katie stayed close to Jainu, her heart pounding with fear. She could feel the darkness closing in around them, trying to drag them down into despair. But she refused to give up—she knew that they had to find a way out of the darkness, to overcome the fear that threatened to consume them.

"We can't let the darkness win," Katie said, her voice filled with determination. "We have to fight back—we have to find the light."

Jainu nodded, his eyes filled with resolve. Together, they focused all their willpower on overcoming the darkness, forcing themselves to keep moving forward, one step at a time.

As they walked, they began to notice something strange. The darkness around them seemed to be reacting to their presence, growing more intense as they fought against it. The shadows shifted and moved, as if they were alive, trying to drag them down into the depths of despair.

But Jainu refused to let the darkness win. He focused all his willpower on finding the light, forcing himself to remember the moments of hope and joy that had kept him going during the darkest times of his life.

"We control the darkness—not the labyrinth!" Jainu shouted, his voice filled with determination.

Katie nodded, her eyes filled with resolve. Together, they focused their willpower on finding the light, forcing the darkness to retreat. The forest around them began to change, the shadows fading as they reclaimed their memories.

Finally, the darkness disappeared, replaced by the glowing chamber they had been in before. The crystal in the center of the chamber pulsed gently, its light a reminder of the power they now held.

"We did it," Katie whispered, her voice filled with awe. "We overcame the darkness."

Jainu nodded, his heart pounding with a mixture of relief and pride. "But the labyrinth isn't done with us yet. There's still one more trial to come."

The Final Revelation

The air around them shimmered, and they were transported to a new memory—one that was filled with light and warmth.

They found themselves standing in a sunlit meadow, the air filled with the scent of blooming flowers and the sound of birds singing. The sky was a brilliant shade of blue, and the sun shone down warmly on their faces.

"This is… this is the place where I found hope," Jainu whispered, his voice filled with emotion. "This is where I realized that I could overcome anything."

Katie stared at the scene before them, her heart filled with awe. The memory was so vivid that it was as if they had been transported back to that very moment, to the day when they had found the strength to keep going, no matter what.

"This is... beautiful," Katie said, her voice filled with awe. "But why is the labyrinth showing us this?"

Jainu shook his head, his mind racing. "I don't know... but I think it's trying to remind us of something. Something important."

As they walked through the meadow, the memory began to shift and change, showing them moments from their journey together—moments of hope and joy, of love and friendship. The labyrinth was reminding them of the bond they shared, of the strength they had found in each other as they faced the trials of the forest together.

"This is... incredible," Katie whispered, her voice filled with emotion. "The labyrinth is showing us our journey—our story."

Jainu nodded, his eyes filled with tears. "It's reminding us of why we're here—of what we're fighting for."

As they continued through the meadow, the memory began to fade, replaced by the glowing chamber they had been in before. The crystal in the center of the chamber pulsed gently, its light a reminder of the power they now held.

"We've faced our fears, our regrets, our love, and our darkness," Katie said, her voice filled with determination. "But what's next? What more does the labyrinth want from us?"

Jainu stared at the crystal, his mind racing. "I don't know... but whatever it is, we'll face it together."

The air around them shimmered, and they were transported to a new memory—one that was filled with light and warmth.

They found themselves standing in a sunlit meadow, the air filled with the scent of blooming flowers and the sound of birds singing. The sky was a brilliant shade of blue, and the sun shone down warmly on their faces.

"This is... this is the place where I found hope," Jainu whispered, his voice filled with emotion. "This is where I realized that I could overcome anything."

Katie stared at the scene before them, her heart filled with awe. The memory was so vivid that it was as if they had been transported back to that very moment, to the day when they had found the strength to keep going, no matter what.

"This is... beautiful," Katie said, her voice filled with awe. "But why is the labyrinth showing us this?"

Jainu shook his head, his mind racing. "I don't know... but I think it's trying to remind us of something. Something important."

As they walked through the meadow, the memory began to shift and change, showing them moments from their journey together—moments of hope and joy, of love and friendship. The labyrinth was reminding them of the bond they shared, of the strength they had found in each other as they faced the trials of the forest together.

"This is... incredible," Katie whispered, her voice filled with emotion. "The labyrinth is showing us our journey—our story."

Jainu nodded, his eyes filled with tears. "It's reminding us of why we're here—of what we're fighting for."

As they continued through the meadow, the memory began to fade, replaced by the glowing chamber they had been in before. The crystal in the center of the chamber pulsed gently, its light a reminder of the power they now held.

"We've faced our fears, our regrets, our love, and our darkness," Katie said, her voice filled with determination. "But what's next? What more does the labyrinth want from us?"

Jainu stared at the crystal, his mind racing. "I don't know… but whatever it is, we'll face it together."

Chapter 5

The Guardians' Path

The labyrinth had tested them in ways they had never imagined, pushing them to confront their darkest fears and deepest regrets. Yet, it was also a place of incredible beauty, filled with ancient magic and hidden secrets that had been locked away for centuries. As Jainu and Katie emerged from the maze, they found themselves standing on the edge of a vast expanse, the ground beneath their feet giving way to rolling hills and distant mountains that stretched as far as the eye could see.

The air here was different—crisper, filled with the scent of pine and the distant sound of flowing water. It was as if they had stepped into another world, one that was untouched by time and filled with the promise of discovery.

Katie took a deep breath, her eyes scanning the horizon. "This place... it's beautiful."

Jainu nodded, his gaze fixed on the distant mountains. "It's like the forest is opening up to us, showing us its true nature."

They stood in silence for a moment, taking in the breathtaking view. The trials of the labyrinth had left them both physically and emotionally exhausted, but there was also a sense of accomplishment that filled the air between them. They had faced their fears, confronted their pasts, and come out stronger on the other side.

But they both knew that their journey was far from over.

"The labyrinth was just the beginning," Jainu said quietly, his voice filled with determination. "There's more we need to do—more we need to discover."

Katie nodded, her expression serious. "And we'll do it together."

They began to walk across the open expanse, the ground beneath their feet soft and covered in wildflowers that swayed gently in the breeze. The sun was beginning to set, casting long shadows across the landscape and bathing everything in a warm, golden light.

As they walked, they talked about the labyrinth and the memories they had faced within its twisting corridors. They shared stories of their pasts, of the moments that had shaped them into the people they were today. There was a sense of closeness between them, a bond that had been forged in the fires of the labyrinth and strengthened by their shared experiences.

"I never thought I'd have to face those memories again," Katie admitted, her voice soft as she looked down at the flowers beneath her feet. "But I'm glad I did. It was painful, but it also helped me see things more clearly."

Jainu glanced at her, his expression thoughtful. "The labyrinth was trying to teach us something—to make us stronger, more resilient. It was a test, but also a lesson."

Katie nodded, a small smile playing on her lips. "And we passed."

As they continued to walk, the landscape began to change. The rolling hills gave way to dense forests, the trees towering above them like ancient guardians.

The path they were following grew narrower, winding through the trees in a serpentine pattern that made it difficult to see what lay ahead.

The forest was alive with the sounds of nature—the chirping of birds, the rustle of leaves in the breeze, the distant call of animals hidden within the underbrush. It was a place of beauty, but also of mystery, and there was a sense of anticipation that hung in the air, as if the forest itself was aware of their presence and was watching them closely.

"Do you think we'll find more trials here?" Katie asked, her voice barely above a whisper as she looked around at the towering trees.

Jainu nodded, his expression serious. "The forest is testing us—guiding us to something. Whatever it is, we need to be ready."

They continued to walk in silence, the path before them growing darker as the sun dipped below the horizon. The trees closed in around them, their branches intertwining above to form a canopy that blocked out the remaining light. The air grew cooler, and the sounds of the forest seemed to grow louder, more intense.

Suddenly, they heard a low growl coming from the shadows ahead. Jainu and Katie stopped in their tracks, their hearts pounding as they strained to see what was lurking in the darkness.

The growl grew louder, closer, and then, without warning, a massive creature leaped out of the shadows, its eyes glowing with a malevolent light. It was a beast unlike anything they had ever seen—its body covered in dark, matted fur, its claws sharp and gleaming in the dim light.

Jainu reacted instinctively, drawing his sword and stepping in front of Katie to protect her. "Stay behind me!"

The beast snarled, its eyes locked on Jainu as it prepared to pounce. But before it could make its move, the ground beneath it began to tremble, and thick vines erupted from the earth, wrapping around the creature's legs and pulling it to the ground.

Katie gasped, her eyes wide as she watched the vines tighten around the beast, immobilizing it. "The forest... it's protecting us."

Jainu nodded, his grip on his sword relaxing slightly. "It seems the forest wants us to continue our journey."

The beast struggled against the vines, snarling and snapping its jaws, but it was unable to break free. Jainu and Katie took the opportunity to move past it, carefully stepping around the thrashing creature and continuing down the path.

As they walked, the forest began to change once again. The trees grew taller and more ancient, their bark covered in thick layers of moss and lichen. The air grew warmer, filled with the scent of blooming flowers and the soft hum of insects.

They soon came to a clearing, where the trees parted to reveal a large, shimmering pool of water. The surface of the pool was perfectly still, reflecting the sky above like a mirror. At the center of the pool was a small island, covered in lush greenery and vibrant flowers.

"This place... it's beautiful," Katie whispered, her voice filled with awe as she gazed at the tranquil scene before them.

Jainu nodded, his expression thoughtful. "It feels peaceful here... but there's something more. I can feel it."

They approached the edge of the pool, their reflections staring back at them from the water's surface. The air around them was filled with a sense of calm, but also of anticipation, as if the pool was waiting for them to take the next step.

"What do you think we're supposed to do?" Katie asked, her eyes fixed on the island at the center of the pool.

Jainu studied the scene before them, his mind racing. "There's something on that island—something important. I think we need to find a way to reach it."

They looked around the clearing, searching for anything that might help them cross the water. There were no boats or bridges, and the water was too deep to wade through.

Katie frowned, her brow furrowed in concentration. "Maybe there's another way... something we're not seeing."

Jainu nodded, his gaze scanning the surrounding trees. "The forest has been guiding us so far—maybe it will show us the way."

They stood in silence, their senses attuned to the magic of the forest. The air was thick with the scent of flowers, and the soft hum of insects filled their ears. But there was something more—a faint, almost imperceptible energy that pulsed through the ground, like the heartbeat of the earth itself.

Then, without warning, the water at the edge of the pool began to ripple, and a small, glowing stone emerged from the depths. The stone floated to the surface, its light reflecting off the water and casting shimmering patterns on the trees around them.

Katie reached out to touch the stone, her fingers brushing against its cool, smooth surface. The moment she made contact, the stone flared with light, and the water around it began to glow with a soft, golden hue.

Jainu and Katie watched in awe as a path of glowing stones appeared, leading from the edge of the pool to the island at its center. The stones were perfectly spaced, creating a narrow walkway that seemed to float on the surface of the water.

"The forest... it created a path for us," Katie whispered, her voice filled with wonder.

Jainu nodded, his eyes fixed on the glowing stones. "It wants us to reach the island—there's something there that we need to find."

They stepped onto the first stone, the surface cool and solid beneath their feet. The water around them shimmered with light, the reflections dancing like fireflies on the surface.

As they made their way across the pool, the air around them grew warmer, filled with the scent of blooming flowers and the soft hum of insects. The island at the center of the pool seemed to glow with an inner light, beckoning them closer with each step.

When they finally reached the island, they found themselves standing in a small, lush garden, filled with vibrant flowers and towering trees. The air was thick with the scent of jasmine and roses, and the ground beneath their feet was soft with moss and grass.

In the center of the garden was a large, ancient tree, its bark rough and weathered with age. The tree's branches stretched high above them, casting dappled shadows on the ground below. At the base of the tree was a small, stone pedestal, its surface covered in intricate carvings that glowed faintly in the dim light.

"This tree... it feels ancient," Katie said, her voice filled with awe as she approached the pedestal. "Like it's been here for centuries."

Jainu nodded, his eyes scanning the carvings on the pedestal. "

The magic here is strong—this tree is connected to the forest in a way we don't fully understand."

They examined the pedestal, their fingers tracing the intricate carvings. The symbols were unlike anything they had seen before, swirling patterns that seemed to shift and change as they watched.

"This must be another test," Katie said, her voice thoughtful. "But what are we supposed to do?"

Jainu studied the carvings, his mind racing. "I think we need to unlock the magic of the tree— just like we did with the labyrinth. But we have to be careful—the magic here is powerful, and we don't know what might happen if we don't do this correctly."

Katie nodded, her expression serious. "I'll follow your lead."

Jainu reached out to touch the pedestal, his fingers brushing against the cool stone. The moment he made contact, the carvings flared with light, and the ground beneath their feet began to tremble.

They stepped back as the tree's branches began to sway, the leaves rustling in the breeze. The air around them grew warmer, and the scent of flowers intensified, filling their senses with the heady aroma.

Suddenly, the tree's bark began to glow, the light spreading out in ripples across its surface. The ground around the tree cracked and shifted, revealing a hidden chamber beneath the roots.

Katie gasped, her eyes wide as she stared at the opening in the ground. "There's something down there... something hidden."

Jainu nodded, his heart pounding with anticipation. "This must be what the forest wanted us to find."

They carefully descended into the hidden chamber, the air growing cooler as they moved deeper underground. The walls of the chamber were lined with ancient stone, covered in the same intricate carvings they had seen on the pedestal.

At the center of the chamber was a large, glowing crystal, its light pulsing gently in the darkness. The crystal was surrounded by a circle of stones, each one covered in the same swirling symbols.

"This is incredible," Katie whispered, her voice filled with awe as she gazed at the glowing crystal. "But what is it?"

Jainu studied the crystal, his mind racing. "It's a source of power—an ancient magic that has been hidden away for centuries. The forest has been guiding us to this point, leading us to unlock this power."

Katie reached out to touch the crystal, but before she could make contact, the air around them began to shimmer, and the walls of the chamber started to shift and change.

They found themselves standing in a vast, open landscape, the ground beneath their feet soft and covered in wildflowers. The sky above was a brilliant shade of blue, and the sun shone down warmly on their faces.

"This... this is a memory," Jainu realized, his voice filled with shock. "But whose memory is it?"

Katie looked around, her eyes wide with wonder. "It's beautiful... but there's something familiar about this place."

As they walked through the landscape, the memory began to shift and change, showing them scenes from the past—moments of joy and sorrow, of triumph and defeat. The memory was so vivid that it was as if they were living through it all over again.

Suddenly, they heard a voice—a deep, resonant voice that seemed to echo from the very earth beneath their feet.

"Who are you, travelers, who seek to unlock the power of the forest?"

Jainu and Katie exchanged a glance, their hearts pounding in their chests. The voice was ancient, filled with a wisdom that spanned centuries.

"We are travelers on a quest," Jainu called out, his voice steady. "We seek to unlock the secrets of the forest and discover the power that lies within."

There was a moment of silence, and then the voice spoke again, filled with a sense of purpose.

"Many have sought the power of the forest, but few have been worthy. To unlock the power, you must first prove yourselves—face the trials of the Guardians, and only then will the power be revealed to you."

Jainu and Katie felt a surge of determination. They had faced the trials of the labyrinth and overcome their darkest fears. Whatever the Guardians had in store for them, they were ready.

"We accept the challenge," Jainu declared, his voice filled with resolve.

The landscape around them began to shift and change once again, the ground beneath their feet trembling as the memory faded away.

When the world came back into focus, they found themselves standing in a large, circular chamber. The walls were lined with ancient stone, covered in intricate carvings that glowed faintly in the dim light. The air was thick with the scent of incense, and the soft hum of magic filled their ears.

At the center of the chamber stood three tall figures, their bodies cloaked in shadow. They were the Guardians—ancient beings who had been entrusted with protecting the secrets of the forest for centuries.

"Welcome, travelers," one of the Guardians spoke, his voice deep and resonant. "You have journeyed far and faced many trials, but your journey is not yet complete. To unlock the power of the forest, you must first prove yourselves worthy."

The Guardians stepped forward, their forms becoming more distinct as they emerged from the shadows. They were tall and imposing, their bodies covered in intricate armor that shimmered in the dim light. Each Guardian held a weapon—a sword, a staff, and a shield—symbols of their power and authority.

"The first trial," the Guardian with the sword spoke, his voice filled with authority. "Is the Trial of

Strength. You must face the challenges of the physical world and prove your strength and courage."

The second Guardian, holding the staff, stepped forward. "The second trial is the Trial of Wisdom. You must solve the riddles of the ancient world and prove your knowledge and understanding."

The third Guardian, holding the shield, stepped forward. "The final trial is the Trial of the Heart. You must confront your deepest fears and desires, and prove the purity of your heart."

Jainu and Katie exchanged a glance, their hearts pounding with anticipation. They had come so far, faced so many challenges, and now they were being asked to prove themselves once again.

"We accept the trials," Jainu declared, his voice filled with determination. "We will face them together."

The Guardians nodded, their forms shimmering as they stepped back into the shadows.

"Then let the trials begin," the first Guardian spoke, his voice echoing through the chamber.

The Trial of Strength

The chamber around them began to shift and change, the walls fading away to reveal a vast, open landscape. The ground beneath their feet was hard and rocky, and the air was thick with the scent of sweat and blood.

They found themselves standing in a large arena, the ground beneath their feet covered in sand. The arena was surrounded by towering walls, and the sound of cheering filled the air as an unseen crowd roared with excitement.

"This... this is a battlefield," Katie realized, her voice filled with shock.

Jainu nodded, his grip tightening on his sword. "The Trial of Strength. We have to prove our courage and our ability to fight."

Suddenly, the ground beneath their feet began to tremble, and the air was filled with the sound of clashing swords and the cries of battle. Figures emerged from the shadows—warriors clad in armor, their weapons gleaming in the dim light.

The warriors charged at them, their eyes filled with a fierce determination. Jainu and Katie reacted instinctively, raising their weapons to defend themselves.

The battle was fierce and intense, the warriors attacking with a relentless fury. Jainu and Katie fought side by side, their movements swift and precise as they cut down their enemies one by one.

But the Trial of Strength was not just a test of physical ability—it was also a test of endurance. The warriors kept coming, their attacks growing more powerful and more coordinated as the battle raged on.

Jainu could feel his strength beginning to wane, his muscles aching from the strain of the fight. But he refused to give up—he knew that they had to prove themselves worthy if they were to unlock the power of the forest.

Katie fought with all her might, her heart pounding in her chest as she parried blow after blow. She could feel the weight of the trial bearing down on her, but she refused to let it break her.

Finally, after what felt like hours of fighting, the last of the warriors fell to the ground, their bodies dissolving into shadows as the battle came to an end.

Jainu and Katie stood panting, their bodies covered in sweat and blood. The arena around them began to fade away, replaced by the familiar walls of the chamber.

The first Guardian stepped forward, his voice filled with approval. "You have proven your strength and courage. The Trial of Strength is complete."

Jainu and Katie exchanged a glance, their hearts filled with a sense of accomplishment. They had passed the first trial, but they knew that the hardest challenges were still to come.

The Trial of Wisdom

The second Guardian stepped forward, his staff glowing with a soft, golden light. "The next trial is the Trial of Wisdom. You must solve the riddles of the ancient world and prove your knowledge and understanding."

The chamber around them began to shift and change once again, the walls fading away to reveal a vast library. The air was thick with the scent of old books and parchment, and the soft glow of candlelight illuminated the rows of shelves that stretched as far as the eye could see.

Jainu and Katie found themselves standing in the center of the library, surrounded by ancient tomes and scrolls. The air was filled with the soft rustle of pages, as if the books themselves were alive, whispering secrets of the past.

"This place... it's incredible," Katie whispered, her voice filled with awe as she gazed at the rows of books. "But how are we supposed to solve the riddles?"

Jainu studied the books around them, his mind racing. "The answers are here—hidden within the texts. We just need to find them."

They began to search through the library, pulling books from the shelves and scanning the pages for any clues. The books were filled with ancient knowledge, their pages covered in intricate symbols and diagrams.

But the Trial of Wisdom was not just a test of knowledge—it was also a test of understanding. The riddles they were faced with were complex and multilayered, requiring them to think beyond the surface and delve into the deeper meanings of the texts.

As they worked through the riddles, they were forced to confront their own beliefs and assumptions, questioning everything they thought they knew about the world. The Trial of Wisdom was not just about finding the right answers—it was about expanding their minds and opening themselves up to new possibilities.

Finally, after hours of searching and deciphering, they found the answers they were looking for. The riddles were solved, and the knowledge they had gained was more than just intellectual—it was a deeper understanding of the world and their place within it.

The library around them began to fade away, replaced by the familiar walls of the chamber.

The second Guardian stepped forward, his voice filled with approval. "You have proven your knowledge and understanding. The Trial of Wisdom is complete."

Jainu and Katie exchanged a glance, their hearts filled with a sense of accomplishment. They had passed the second trial, but they knew that the final challenge would be the most difficult of all.

The Trial of the Heart

The third Guardian stepped forward, his shield glowing with a soft, golden light. "The final trial is the Trial of the Heart. You must confront your deepest fears and desires, and prove the purity of your heart."

The chamber around them began to shift and change once again, the walls fading away to reveal a vast, open landscape. The ground beneath their feet was soft and covered in wildflowers, and the air was filled with the scent of blooming flowers and the sound of birds singing.

They found themselves standing in a sunlit meadow, the sky above a brilliant shade of blue. The scene was peaceful and serene, but there was a sense of anticipation in the air, as if something was waiting for them just beyond the horizon.

"This place... it's beautiful," Katie whispered, her voice filled with awe as she gazed at the meadow around them.

Jainu nodded, his expression thoughtful. "But this is the Trial of the Heart. There must be something more."

As they walked through the meadow, the landscape began to shift and change, showing them scenes from their pasts—moments of joy and sorrow, of love and loss. The Trial of the Heart was not just about confronting their fears—it was about confronting their deepest desires and the choices they had made along the way.

They were forced to relive moments of pain and regret, to question the decisions they had made and the paths they had chosen. The Trial of the Heart was a test of their inner strength, of their ability to face the truth about themselves and their deepest emotions.

But it was also a test of love. The Trial of the Heart forced them to confront the bond they shared, to question the depth of their feelings for each other and the choices they had made in their journey together.

As they faced the final challenge, they were forced to make a choice—a choice that would determine their fate and the fate of the forest.

The Trial of the Heart was not just about proving their worth—it was about proving their love and their commitment to each other and to the journey they had undertaken.

Finally, after what felt like hours of soul-searching and introspection, they emerged from the Trial of the Heart stronger and more united than ever.

The meadow around them began to fade away, replaced by the familiar walls of the chamber.

The third Guardian stepped forward, his voice filled with approval. "You have proven the purity of your heart. The Trial of the Heart is complete."

The Final Revelation

The three Guardians stepped forward, their forms shimmering as they emerged from the shadows.

"You have passed the trials and proven yourselves worthy," the first Guardian spoke, his voice filled with pride. "The power of the forest is now yours."

The chamber around them began to shift and change once again, the walls fading away to reveal a vast, open landscape. The ground beneath their feet was soft and covered in wildflowers, and the air was filled with the scent of blooming flowers and the sound of birds singing.

At the center of the landscape was a large, glowing crystal, its light pulsing gently in the dim light. The crystal was surrounded by a circle of stones, each one covered in intricate carvings that glowed faintly in the darkness.

"This is the heart of the forest," the second Guardian spoke, his voice filled with reverence. "The source of the ancient magic that has been hidden away for centuries."

The third Guardian stepped forward, his voice filled with purpose. "The power of the forest is now yours to command. Use it wisely, for it is a power that can create or destroy, depending on how it is wielded."

Jainu and Katie exchanged a glance, their hearts filled with a mixture of awe and determination. They had come so far, faced so many challenges, and now they were being entrusted with the power of the forest—a power that could change the world.

"We will use this power wisely," Jainu declared, his voice filled with resolve. "We will protect the forest and the world from those who would seek to harm it."

The Guardians nodded, their forms shimmering as they began to fade away.

"Your journey is not yet complete," the first Guardian spoke, his voice growing fainter. "There are still challenges ahead, but you are now prepared to face them."

The Guardians disappeared, leaving Jainu and Katie standing alone in the vast, open landscape.

They approached the glowing crystal, their hearts pounding with anticipation. The crystal's light pulsed gently, filling the air with a sense of calm and peace.

Jainu reached out to touch the crystal, his fingers brushing against its cool, smooth surface. The moment he made contact, the crystal flared with light, and the air around them was filled with a blinding brilliance.

They felt a surge of power course through them, as if the magic of the forest was flowing into their very beings. The crystal's light filled them with a sense of purpose and determination, a reminder of the responsibility they now held.

As the light began to fade, Jainu and Katie opened their eyes, their hearts still pounding with the intensity of the experience. The crystal in their hands was now cool, its light dimmed, but the connection they felt with the forest remained strong.

"We did it," Katie whispered, her voice filled with awe. "We unlocked the power of the forest."

Jainu nodded, his heart pounding with a mixture of excitement and awe. "But this is just the beginning.

There's so much more to discover, so much more to learn."

Katie looked at him, her eyes filled with determination. "Then let's keep going. Let's find out what the forest has in store for us."

They left the chamber, the crystal in hand guiding their way. The path ahead was long and winding, but they were no longer afraid. The forest was alive with magic, and they were a part of it, connected to its ancient power in a way that few people ever would be.

As they walked, they could feel the forest responding to their presence, the trees swaying gently in the breeze, the animals watching them from the shadows. It was as if the forest itself was guiding them, showing them the way forward.

They came across more ancient stone pillars, each one covered in the same intricate carvings they had seen before. The symbols on the pillars glowed faintly, their light guiding them through the dense underbrush.

"This forest is incredible," Katie said, her voice filled with awe as she took in the sights around them. "It's like it's alive, like it's watching over us."

Jainu nodded, his eyes scanning the trees around them. "It is alive. The magic here... it's connected to everything in the forest. We're just a part of it, a small piece of a much larger puzzle."

They continued walking, the path beneath their feet becoming more defined as they ventured deeper into the forest. The air was thick with magic, the power of the forest pulsing around them like a living presence.

After several hours of walking, they came across a small stream, its water crystal clear and shimmering with a soft, golden light. The stream's banks were lined with flowers, their petals glowing in the sunlight, and the air was filled with the gentle sound of the water flowing over the rocks.

Jainu and Katie knelt by the stream, their hands cupped to drink the cool, refreshing water. As they drank, they felt the magic of the forest flowing through them, filling them with a sense of peace and renewal.

"This water... it's like nothing I've ever tasted before," Katie said, her voice filled with wonder. "It's like it's alive, filled with the magic of the forest."

Jainu nodded, feeling the same sense of awe. "It is. This whole forest... it's alive, filled with magic. And we're a part of it now."

They continued on, following the stream as it wound its way through the forest. The path was lined with more flowers, their petals glowing in the sunlight, and the air was filled with the scent of blooming blossoms.

As they walked, they noticed more signs of the forest's magic. They came across a grove of trees, their trunks twisted and gnarled, their branches intertwined to form a dense canopy overhead. The light filtering through the leaves cast a soft, golden glow over the grove, and the air was filled with the scent of pine and earth.

In the center of the grove stood a small stone altar, similar to the ones they

had seen before, but this one was different. The altar was covered in intricate carvings, the symbols glowing faintly in the dim light. The air around the altar was thick with magic, and Jainu and Katie could feel its power resonating in the air around them.

They approached the altar cautiously, their steps slow and reverent. The magic here was strong, more powerful than anything they had felt before, and they knew that they were standing in a place of great significance.

"This altar... it feels different from the others," Katie said, her voice hushed. "The magic here is stronger, more intense."

Jainu nodded, feeling the same sense of awe. "It's like the forest is guiding us here, showing us something important."

As they stood before the altar, the symbols began to glow brighter, their light spreading out in ripples across the surface of the stone. The air around them hummed with energy, and Jainu could feel the magic of the forest resonating with the altar, unlocking the ancient power that lay within.

For a moment, they stood in silence, the light from the symbols surrounding them, the magic of the altar flowing through them. It was a moment of pure connection, of unity with the forest and its ancient power.

Then, as the light began to fade, Jainu and Katie opened their eyes, their hearts still filled with the warmth of the magic. The crystal in Jainu's hand was now cool, its light dimmed, but the connection they felt with the forest remained strong.

"Do you think the magic will guide us to where we need to go next?" Katie asked, her voice filled with wonder.

Jainu nodded, his gaze still on the altar. "I believe so. This forest... it's more than just a place. It's like a living entity, and it wants to protect its secrets. But now that we've unlocked this part of its magic, I think it will guide us to the next step."

Katie smiled, her heart swelling with the possibilities of what lay ahead. "I can't wait to see what comes next."

As they left the grove and continued their journey, they felt a renewed sense of purpose. The forest was alive with magic, and they were connected to it in a way that few had ever been. The path before them was long and filled with unknown challenges, but they knew they would face whatever came their way together.

Chapter 6

The Trial of
the Eternal Flame

The Journey to the Heart of the Forest

The air grew denser with magic as Jainu and Katie ventured deeper into the forest. Each step felt like a journey through time itself, the weight of the ancient trees pressing down on them, as if the forest was alive and watching their every move. The path they had been following seemed to narrow, leading them toward an unknown destination, with the key in Jainu's hand pulsing softly as if guiding them forward.

"This place... it feels different from the rest of the forest," Katie murmured, her eyes scanning the dense foliage around them. "It's like we're walking into the heart of something ancient and powerful."

Jainu nodded, his senses on high alert. "I can feel it too. The magic here is stronger, more intense. Whatever lies ahead, it's going to be unlike anything we've faced before."

They continued walking in silence, the forest around them growing darker as the canopy above thickened, blocking out the light. The trees towered over them, their branches intertwined in a web of greenery that seemed to stretch endlessly into the sky. The air was cool and damp, filled with the scent of earth and decaying leaves, and the only sound was the soft rustle of the wind through the trees.

After what felt like hours of walking, they emerged into a small clearing. In the center of the clearing stood a massive tree, its trunk wider than any they had seen before. The tree's bark was dark and gnarled, covered in thick vines that pulsed with a faint, green light. The branches stretched out like arms, reaching toward the sky, and at the base of the tree was a large, stone altar, its surface covered in intricate carvings.

"This must be the place," Katie whispered, her voice filled with awe as she approached the altar. "The heart of the forest."

Jainu nodded, his eyes fixed on the altar. "It has to be. The key led us here for a reason."

As they stepped closer to the altar, the ground beneath their feet began to tremble, and the air around them grew thick with energy. The carvings on the altar flared with light, and the tree above them seemed to come alive, its branches swaying as if moved by an unseen force.

Suddenly, the air was filled with the sound of a deep, resonant voice, echoing from the very depths of the earth.

"Who dares to enter the heart of the forest?"

Jainu and Katie exchanged a glance, their hearts pounding in their chests. The voice was ancient and powerful, filled with a wisdom that spanned centuries.

"We are travelers on a quest," Jainu called out, his voice steady. "We seek to unlock the secrets of the forest and discover the power that lies within."

There was a moment of silence, and then the voice spoke again, filled with a sense of purpose.

"Many have sought the power of the forest, but few have been worthy. To unlock the power, you must first prove yourselves—face the Trial of the Eternal Flame, and only then will the power be revealed to you."

Jainu and Katie felt a surge of determination. They had faced countless trials and challenges, and they were ready to prove themselves once again.

"We accept the trial," Jainu declared, his voice filled with resolve. "We will face it together."

The ground beneath their feet began to tremble more violently, and the air around them shimmered with energy. The altar flared with light, and the tree above them seemed to pulse with power. Then, with a sudden burst of energy, the world around them shifted, and they were transported to a new location.

The Realm of the Eternal Flame

They found themselves standing in a vast, open landscape, the ground beneath their feet covered in blackened ash and scorched earth. The sky above was a deep, fiery red, and the air was thick with the scent of smoke and burning wood. In the distance, they could see a massive volcano, its peak spewing molten lava into the air.

"This place... it feels like we're standing on the edge of the world," Katie whispered, her voice filled with awe and fear.

Jainu nodded, his eyes scanning the horizon. "This is the Realm of the Eternal Flame. The trial begins here."

They began to walk across the barren landscape, the ground crunching beneath their feet as they moved closer to the volcano. The air grew hotter with each step, the heat from the molten lava searing their skin and making it difficult to breathe. But they pressed on, determined to prove themselves worthy of the power they sought.

As they approached the base of the volcano, they saw a figure standing in their path. The figure was tall and imposing, clad in armor that glowed with a fiery light. In its hand, it held a massive sword, its blade shimmering with heat.

"Who are you?" Katie called out, her voice trembling with fear and determination.

The figure turned to face them, its eyes glowing with a fierce, red light. "I am the Guardian of the Eternal Flame," it declared, its voice deep and resonant. "To pass the trial, you must defeat me in combat."

Jainu stepped forward, his hand on the hilt of his sword. "We accept your challenge," he said, his voice filled with determination.

The Guardian raised its sword, the blade crackling with energy. "Then prepare yourselves, for only the strong shall survive."

The battle that followed was fierce and intense. The Guardian attacked with relentless fury, its sword blazing with the power of the Eternal Flame. Jainu and Katie fought side by side, their movements swift and precise as they parried the Guardian's attacks and struck back with their own.

The heat from the Guardian's sword was almost unbearable, the flames licking at their skin and threatening to consume them. But they refused to give up, pushing themselves to their limits as they fought with all their might.

Finally, after what felt like an eternity, Jainu saw an opening. He lunged forward, his sword slicing through the air and striking the Guardian's armor with a resounding crash. The Guardian staggered back, its sword dropping to the ground as it let out a roar of pain and anger.

Katie seized the opportunity, raising her own sword and striking the Guardian with all her strength. The Guardian let out one final roar before its body was consumed by flames, the fiery light fading as it crumbled to the ground in a pile of ash.

Jainu and Katie stood panting, their bodies covered in sweat and soot. The ground beneath them began to tremble, and the air was filled with the sound of cracking stone. The volcano before them erupted with a deafening roar, sending a torrent of lava cascading down its slopes.

"We need to get out of here!" Katie shouted, her voice filled with urgency.

Jainu nodded, grabbing her hand and pulling her away from the volcano. They ran as fast as they could, the ground shaking beneath their feet as the lava flowed toward them. The heat was intense, the air filled with ash and smoke that choked their lungs.

But just as the lava was about to overtake them, the ground beneath their feet gave way, and they were plunged into darkness.

The Caverns of Reflection

When Jainu and Katie awoke, they found themselves lying on the cold, hard ground of a dark cavern. The air was damp and musty, filled with the sound of dripping water. The only light came from the faint glow of the key in Jainu's hand, casting eerie shadows on the walls around them.

"Where are we?" Katie asked, her voice trembling as she sat up and looked around.

Jainu shook his head, his mind still foggy from the ordeal. "I'm not sure... but it seems we've passed the first part of the trial."

They got to their feet, their bodies aching from the battle and the fall. The cavern was vast, the walls covered in jagged rocks and stalactites that hung from the ceiling like the teeth of a giant beast. The air was cool, a stark contrast to the fiery heat of the Realm of the Eternal Flame.

As they began to explore the cavern, they noticed that the walls were covered in strange, glowing symbols. The symbols seemed to pulse with a faint light, casting an ethereal glow on the rocks around them.

"What do you think these symbols mean?" Katie asked, her voice filled with curiosity as she traced the patterns with her fingers.

Jainu studied the symbols, his mind racing. "They seem familiar... like something we've seen before. But I'm not sure what they mean."

They continued walking through the cavern, the path winding through narrow tunnels and vast chambers filled with strange rock formations. The symbols on the walls grew more intricate and complex as they went, the light they emitted growing brighter and more intense.

Finally, they reached a large chamber at the heart of the cavern. The walls were covered in symbols that glowed with a bright, golden light, illuminating the entire room. In the center of the chamber stood a large, stone pedestal, its surface covered in the same intricate carvings they had seen before.

"This must be another part of the trial," Katie said, her voice filled with awe as she approached the pedestal.

Jainu nodded, his eyes fixed on the carvings. "The Trial of the Eternal Flame isn't just about strength—it's about reflection and understanding. We need to unlock the meaning of these symbols."

They examined the carvings on the pedestal, their minds racing as they tried to decipher the meaning of the symbols. The patterns were complex and layered, each one representing a different aspect of the trial they were facing.

As they worked, they began to see connections between the symbols and the experiences they had faced on their journey. The symbols represented their struggles, their fears, and their triumphs. They were a reflection of the challenges they had overcome and the lessons they had learned along the way.

Finally, after hours of study and reflection, they unlocked the meaning of the symbols. The carvings on the pedestal flared with light, and the ground beneath their feet began to tremble.

The walls of the cavern shifted and changed, the symbols fading away as the chamber was bathed in a bright, golden light. The air was filled with a sense of peace and calm, a stark contrast to the chaos and danger they had faced in the Realm of the Eternal Flame.

"We did it," Katie whispered, her voice filled with awe. "We unlocked the meaning of the trial."

Jainu nodded, his heart filled with a sense of accomplishment. "But there's still more to come. The trial isn't over yet."

The River of Memories

As the light from the cavern began to fade, Jainu and Katie found themselves standing on the banks of a wide, flowing river. The water was crystal clear, shimmering with a soft, golden light as it flowed gently over smooth stones. The air was cool and refreshing, filled with the scent of fresh water and blooming flowers.

"This place... it's beautiful," Katie whispered, her eyes wide with wonder as she gazed at the river.

Jainu nodded, his expression thoughtful. "But there's something more here—something we need to discover."

They followed the riverbank, their footsteps soft on the grassy ground. The river flowed smoothly, its surface reflecting the sky above like a mirror. But as they walked, they began to notice something strange.

The water of the river seemed to shift and change, the reflections on its surface transforming into images from their past. They saw scenes from their journey together—moments of triumph and despair, of laughter and sorrow.

"This river... it's showing us our memories," Katie realized, her voice filled with awe.

Jainu nodded, his eyes fixed on the water. "The trial isn't just about reflection—it's about understanding our past and how it has shaped us."

As they continued to walk along the riverbank, the memories grew more vivid and intense. The water showed them scenes from their childhoods, from their early adventures, and from the moments that had defined their lives.

They saw themselves as they had been—young and inexperienced, filled with dreams and fears. They saw the people they had loved and lost, the choices they had made, and the paths they had taken.

The river seemed to flow with the currents of their lives, carrying them along on a journey of self-discovery and reflection. It was a journey that forced them to confront their past, to relive their most painful memories, and to understand the choices that had led them to where they were now.

As they walked, they began to see patterns in the memories—connections between their past experiences and the challenges they had faced on their journey. The river was showing them how their past had shaped their present, and how the choices they had made had led them to this moment.

Finally, after what felt like hours of walking, they reached a small waterfall at the end of the river. The water cascaded down in a gentle stream, pooling in a clear, still pond at the base of the falls.

"This must be the end of the river," Katie said, her voice filled with a sense of calm.

Jainu nodded, his heart filled with a sense of peace. "And the end of this part of the trial."

They knelt by the edge of the pond, their reflections staring back at them from the still water. The air was filled with a sense of tranquility, the sound of the waterfall a soothing presence.

As they gazed into the water, they saw their reflections shift and change, transforming into the images of the people they had become. They saw themselves as they were now—stronger, wiser, and more united than ever before.

"The trial has shown us our past," Jainu said quietly, his voice filled with understanding. "But it's also shown us how far we've come and how much we've grown."

Katie nodded, her eyes filled with tears. "We've faced so many challenges, but we've done it together. And that's what makes us strong."

They sat in silence for a moment, their hearts filled with a sense of gratitude and reflection. The trial had forced them to confront their past, but it had also given them the strength to move forward, to continue their journey with renewed determination.

Finally, they rose to their feet, their hearts filled with resolve.

"The trial isn't over yet," Jainu said, his voice filled with determination. "But we've come this far, and we won't give up now."

Katie nodded, her expression filled with determination. "Let's keep going. We can do this."

The Temple of the Eternal Flame

The path ahead of them led through a dense forest, the trees towering above them like ancient sentinels. The air was thick with the scent of pine and earth, and the soft rustle of leaves filled their ears as they made their way deeper into the woods.

The forest was alive with the magic of the trial, the energy of the Eternal Flame pulsing through the ground beneath their feet. The trees seemed to lean in closer, their branches forming a protective canopy overhead, as if the forest itself was guiding them toward their destination.

After hours of walking, they finally emerged from the forest and found themselves standing before a massive stone temple. The temple was ancient, its walls covered in intricate carvings that glowed faintly in the dim light. The air around the temple was thick with the scent of incense, and the soft hum of magic filled their ears as they approached the entrance.

"This is it," Jainu said, his voice filled with awe as he gazed up at the towering structure. "The Temple of the Eternal Flame."

Katie nodded, her heart pounding with anticipation. "This must be the final part of the trial."

They approached the entrance to the temple, the massive stone doors looming before them like the gates to another world. The doors were covered in the same intricate carvings they had seen throughout their journey, the symbols pulsing with a faint, golden light.

Jainu reached out to touch the doors, his fingers brushing against the cool stone. The moment he made contact, the doors began to tremble, and the air around them was filled with a deep, resonant hum.

With a low groan, the doors slowly began to open, revealing a dark, cavernous interior. The air inside was cool and damp, filled with the scent of earth and stone. The only light came from the faint glow of the symbols on the walls, casting eerie shadows on the floor as they stepped inside.

The interior of the temple was vast, the walls lined with towering stone pillars that seemed to stretch endlessly into the darkness above. The air was thick with the energy of the Eternal Flame, the magic pulsing through the stone like a living presence.

As they made their way deeper into the temple, they came across a large, circular chamber at the heart of the structure. In the center of the chamber was a massive, stone altar, its surface covered in intricate carvings that glowed with a bright, golden light.

"This must be the heart of the temple," Katie whispered, her voice filled with awe as she approached the altar.

Jainu nodded, his eyes fixed on the carvings. "And the final part of the trial."

They examined the carvings on the altar, their minds racing as they tried to decipher the meaning of the symbols. The patterns were complex and layered, each one representing a different aspect of the trial they were facing.

As they worked, they began to see connections between the symbols and the experiences they had faced on their journey. The symbols represented their struggles, their fears, and their triumphs. They were a reflection of the challenges they had overcome and the lessons they had learned along the way.

Finally, after hours of study and reflection, they unlocked the meaning of the symbols. The carvings on the altar flared with light, and the ground beneath their feet began to tremble.

The walls of the chamber shifted and changed, the symbols fading away as the room was bathed in a bright, golden light. The air was filled with a sense of peace and calm, a stark contrast to the chaos and danger they had faced in the Realm of the Eternal Flame.

"We did it," Katie whispered, her voice filled with awe. "We unlocked the meaning of the trial."

Jainu nodded, his heart filled with a sense of accomplishment. "But there's still more to come. The trial isn't over yet."

The Final Confrontation

As the light from the chamber began to fade, Jainu and Katie found themselves standing on the edge of a massive, fiery chasm. The ground beneath their feet was cracked and scorched, and the air was thick with the scent of burning stone.

In the center of the chasm stood a towering figure, its body wreathed in flames. The figure was massive and imposing, its eyes glowing with a fierce, red light. In its hand, it held a massive sword, its blade shimmering with heat.

"Who are you?" Jainu called out, his voice steady despite the fear that gripped his heart.

The figure turned to face them, its eyes locked on Jainu with an intensity that made his blood run cold. "I am the Keeper of the Eternal Flame," it declared, its voice deep and resonant. "To pass the final trial, you must defeat me in combat."

Jainu and Katie exchanged a glance, their hearts pounding with anticipation. They had come so far, faced so many challenges, and now they were being asked to prove themselves one last time.

"We accept your challenge," Jainu declared, his voice filled with resolve.

The Keeper raised its sword, the blade crackling with energy. "Then prepare yourselves, for only the strong shall survive."

The battle that followed was unlike anything they had ever experienced. The Keeper attacked with a fury that shook the very earth beneath their feet, its sword blazing with the power of the Eternal Flame. Jainu and Katie fought side by side, their movements swift and precise as they parried the Keeper's attacks and struck back with their own.

The heat from the Keeper's sword was almost unbearable, the flames licking at their skin and threatening to consume them. But they refused to give up, pushing themselves to their limits as they fought with all their might.

Finally, after what felt like an eternity, Jainu saw an opening. He lunged forward, his sword slicing through the air and striking the Keeper's armor with a resounding crash. The Keeper staggered back, its sword dropping to the ground as it let out a roar of pain and anger.

Katie seized the opportunity, raising her own sword and striking the Keeper with all her strength. The Keeper let out one final roar before its body was consumed by flames, the fiery light fading as it crumbled to the ground in a pile of ash.

Jainu and Katie stood panting, their bodies covered in sweat and soot. The ground beneath them began to tremble, and the air was filled with the sound of cracking stone. The chasm before them erupted with a deafening roar, sending a torrent of lava cascading down its sides.

"We need to get out of here!" Katie shouted, her voice filled with urgency.

Jainu nodded, grabbing her hand and pulling her away from the chasm. They ran as fast as they could, the ground shaking beneath their feet as the lava flowed toward them. The heat was intense, the air filled with ash and smoke that choked their lungs.

But just as the lava was about to overtake them, the ground beneath their feet gave way, and they were plunged into darkness.

The Revelation of the Eternal Flame

When Jainu and Katie awoke, they found themselves lying on the cold, hard ground of a dark chamber. The air was damp and musty, filled with the sound of dripping water. The only light came from the faint glow of the key in Jainu's hand, casting eerie shadows on the walls around them.

"Where are we?" Katie asked, her voice trembling as she sat up and looked around.

Jainu shook his head, his mind still foggy from the ordeal. "I'm not sure... but it seems we've passed the final part of the trial."

They got to their feet, their bodies aching from the battle and the fall. The chamber was vast, the walls covered in jagged rocks and stalactites that hung from the ceiling like the teeth of a giant beast. The air was cool, a stark contrast to the fiery heat of the chasm.

As they began to explore the chamber, they noticed that the walls were covered in strange, glowing symbols. The symbols seemed to pulse with a faint light, casting an ethereal glow on the rocks around them.

"What do you think these symbols mean?" Katie asked, her voice filled with curiosity as she traced the patterns with her fingers.

Jainu studied the symbols, his mind racing. "They seem familiar... like something we've seen before. But I'm not sure what they mean."

They continued walking through the chamber, the path winding through narrow tunnels and vast chambers filled with strange rock formations. The symbols on the walls grew more intricate and complex as they went, the light they emitted growing brighter and more intense.

Finally, they reached a large chamber at the heart of the cavern. The walls were covered in symbols that glowed with a bright, golden light, illuminating the entire room. In the center of the chamber stood a large, stone pedestal, its surface covered in the same intricate carvings they had seen before.

"This must be another part of the trial," Katie said, her voice filled with awe as she approached the pedestal.

Jainu nodded, his eyes fixed on the carvings. "The Trial of the Eternal Flame isn't just about strength— it's about reflection and understanding. We need to unlock the meaning of these symbols."

They examined the carvings on the pedestal, their minds racing as they tried to decipher the meaning of the symbols. The patterns were complex and layered, each one representing a different aspect of the trial they were facing.

As they worked, they began to see connections between the symbols and the experiences they had faced on their journey. The symbols represented their struggles, their fears, and their triumphs. They were a reflection of the challenges they had overcome and the lessons they had learned along the way.

Finally, after hours of study and reflection, they unlocked the meaning of the symbols. The carvings on the pedestal flared with light, and the ground beneath their feet began to tremble.

The walls of the chamber shifted and changed, the symbols fading away as the room was bathed in a bright, golden light. The air was filled with a sense of peace and calm, a stark contrast to the chaos and danger they had faced in the chasm.

As the light began to fade, Jainu and Katie opened their eyes, their hearts still pounding with the intensity of the experience. The key in Jainu's hand was now cool, its light dimmed, but the connection they felt with the Eternal Flame remained strong.

"We did it," Katie whispered, her voice filled with awe. "We unlocked the meaning of the trial."

Jainu nodded, his heart filled with a sense of accomplishment. "But there's still more to come. The trial isn't over yet."

The air around them shimmered, and they were transported to a new location—a vast, open landscape bathed in the warm, golden light of the Eternal Flame. The ground beneath their feet was soft and covered in wildflowers, and the air was filled with the scent of blooming flowers and the sound of birds singing.

In the center of the landscape stood a massive, glowing crystal, its light pulsing gently in the dim light. The crystal was surrounded by a circle of stones, each one covered in intricate carvings that glowed faintly in the darkness.

"This is the heart of the Eternal Flame," Jainu realized, his voice filled with awe.

Katie nodded, her eyes wide with wonder. "The source of the ancient magic that has been hidden away for centuries."

They approached the crystal, their hearts pounding with anticipation. The crystal's light pulsed gently, filling the air with a sense of calm and peace.

Jainu reached out to touch the crystal, his fingers brushing against its cool, smooth surface. The moment he made contact, the crystal flared with light, and the air around them was filled with a blinding brilliance.

They felt a surge of power course through them, as if the magic of the Eternal Flame was flowing into their very beings. The crystal's light filled them with a sense of purpose and determination, a reminder of the responsibility they now held.

As the light began to fade, Jainu and Katie opened their eyes, their hearts still pounding with the intensity of the experience. The crystal in their hands was now cool, its light dimmed, but the connection they felt with the Eternal Flame remained strong.

"We did it," Katie whispered, her voice filled with awe. "We unlocked the power of the Eternal Flame."

Jainu nodded, his heart pounding with a mixture of excitement and awe. "But this is just the beginning. There's so much more to discover, so much more to learn."

Katie looked at him, her eyes filled with determination. "Then let's keep going. Let's find out what the Eternal Flame has in store for us."

They left the chamber, the crystal in hand guiding their way. The path ahead was long and winding, but they were no longer afraid. The Eternal Flame was alive with magic, and they were a part of it, connected to its ancient power in a way that few people ever would be.

As they walked, they could feel the forest responding to their presence, the trees swaying gently in the breeze, the animals watching them from the shadows. It was as if the forest itself was guiding them, showing them the way forward.

They came across more ancient stone pillars, each one covered in the same intricate carvings they had seen before. The symbols on the pillars glowed faintly, their light guiding them through the dense underbrush.

"This forest is incredible," Katie said, her voice filled with awe as she took in the sights around them. "It's like it's alive, like it's watching over us."

Jainu nodded, his eyes scanning the trees around them. "It is alive. The magic here... it's connected to everything in the forest. We're just a part of it, a small piece of a much larger puzzle."

They continued walking, the path beneath their feet becoming more defined as they ventured deeper into the forest. The air was thick with magic, the power of the Eternal Flame pulsing around them like a living presence.

After several hours of walking, they came across a small stream, its water crystal clear and shimmering with a soft, golden light. The stream's banks were lined with flowers, their petals glowing in the sunlight, and the air was filled with the gentle sound of the water flowing over the rocks.

Jainu and Katie knelt by the stream, their hands cupped to drink the cool, refreshing water. As they drank, they felt the magic of the forest flowing through them, filling them with a sense of peace and renewal.

"This water... it's like nothing I've ever tasted before," Katie said, her voice filled with wonder. "It's like it's alive, filled with the magic of the forest."

Jainu nodded, feeling the same sense of awe. "It is. This whole forest... it's alive, filled with magic. And we're a part of it now."

They continued on, following the stream as it wound its way through the forest. The path was lined with more flowers, their petals glowing in the sunlight, and the air was filled with the scent of blooming blossoms.

As they walked, they noticed more signs of the forest's magic. They came across a grove of trees, their trunks twisted and gnarled, their branches intertwined to form a dense canopy overhead. The light filtering through the leaves cast a soft, golden glow over the grove, and the air was filled with the scent of pine and earth.

In the center of the grove stood a small stone altar, similar to the ones they had seen before, but this one was different. The altar was covered in intricate carvings, the symbols glowing faintly in the dim light. The air around the altar was thick with magic, and Jainu and Katie could feel its power resonating in the air around them.

They approached the altar cautiously, their steps slow and reverent. The magic here was strong, more powerful than anything they had felt before, and they knew that they were standing in a place of great significance.

"This altar... it feels different from the others," Katie said, her voice hushed. "The magic here is stronger, more intense."

Jainu nodded, feeling the same sense of awe. "It's like the forest is guiding us here, showing us something important."

As they stood before the altar, the symbols began to glow brighter, their light spreading out in ripples across the surface of the stone. The air around them hummed with energy, and Jainu could feel the magic of the forest resonating with the altar, unlocking the ancient power that lay within.

For a moment, they stood in silence, the light from the symbols surrounding them, the magic of the altar flowing through them. It was a moment of pure connection, of unity with the forest and its ancient power.

Then, as the light began to fade, Jainu and Katie opened their eyes, their hearts still filled with the warmth of the magic. The crystal in Jainu's hand was now cool, its light dimmed, but the connection they felt with the Eternal Flame remained strong.

"Do you think the magic will guide us to where we need to go next?" Katie asked, her voice filled with wonder.

Jainu nodded, his gaze still on the altar. "I believe so. This forest... it's more than just a place. It's like a living entity, and it wants to protect its secrets. But now that we've unlocked this part of its magic, I think it will guide us to the next step."

Katie smiled, her heart swelling with the possibilities of what lay ahead. "I can't wait to see what comes next."

As they left the grove and continued their journey, they felt a renewed sense of purpose. The forest was alive with magic, and they were connected to it in a way that few had ever been. The path before them was long and filled with unknown challenges, but they knew they would face whatever came their way together.

The Guardians' Blessing

As they ventured further into the forest, they noticed that the trees around them began to grow taller and more majestic, their branches stretching high into the sky. The light filtering through the leaves cast dappled shadows on the ground, creating a mosaic of light and dark that shifted and changed with every step.

The air was filled with the soft hum of magic, the energy of the Eternal Flame resonating in the very fabric of the forest. It was as if the forest itself was alive, its magic pulsing through the trees and the earth beneath their feet.

After hours of walking, they finally came across a large, open clearing at the heart of the forest. The clearing was surrounded by towering trees, their trunks covered in thick, green moss that glowed softly in the dim light. The ground was carpeted with wildflowers, their petals shimmering in the sunlight.

In the center of the clearing stood a large stone circle, each stone covered in intricate carvings that glowed with a faint, golden light. The air around the circle was thick with magic, the energy of the Eternal Flame pulsing through the stones like a living presence.

"This must be the place," Katie said, her voice filled with awe as she approached the stone circle. "The place where the Guardians will bless us."

Jainu nodded, his heart pounding with anticipation. "The Guardians of the forest... they're the ones who have been guiding us all along. They're the ones who hold the power of the Eternal Flame."

As they stepped into the stone circle, the air around them shimmered, and the light from the stones grew brighter. The ground beneath their feet began to tremble, and the air was filled with the sound of a deep, resonant hum.

Suddenly, the light from the stones flared with a blinding brilliance, and the air around them was filled with a sense of overwhelming power. Jainu and Katie could feel the magic of the Eternal Flame surging through them, filling them with a sense of purpose and determination.

The light began to coalesce in the center of the stone circle, forming into the shapes of three tall, imposing figures. The figures were cloaked in shadow, their forms shimmering with a soft, golden light.

"The Guardians," Katie whispered, her voice filled with awe as she gazed at the figures before them.

The Guardians stepped forward, their forms becoming more distinct as they emerged from the light. They were tall and majestic, their bodies covered in armor that glowed with the power of the Eternal Flame. Each Guardian held a weapon—a sword, a staff, and a shield—symbols of their power and authority.

"Welcome, travelers," the first Guardian spoke, his voice deep and resonant. "You have journeyed far and faced many trials, but your journey is not yet complete."

The second Guardian stepped forward, his staff glowing with a soft, golden light. "The power of the Eternal Flame is now yours to command. Use it wisely, for it is a power that can create or destroy, depending on how it is wielded."

The third Guardian stepped forward, his shield glowing with a soft, golden light. "Your journey is not yet complete. There are still challenges ahead, but you are now prepared to face them. The power of the Eternal Flame will guide you, protect you, and give you the strength to overcome any obstacle."

Jainu and Katie felt a surge of determination as they listened to the words of the Guardians. They had come so far, faced so many challenges, and now they were being entrusted with the power of the Eternal Flame—a power that could change the world.

"We will use this power wisely," Jainu declared, his voice filled with resolve. "We will protect the forest and the world from those who would seek to harm it."

The Guardians nodded, their forms shimmering as they began to fade away.

"Your journey is not yet complete," the first Guardian spoke, his voice growing fainter. "There are still challenges ahead, but you are now prepared to face them."

The Guardians disappeared, leaving Jainu and Katie standing alone in the stone circle.

They felt a renewed sense of purpose as they left the stone circle and continued their journey. The power of the Eternal Flame was now theirs, and they were ready to face whatever challenges lay ahead.

As they walked, they could feel the magic of the forest responding to their presence, the trees swaying gently in the breeze, the animals watching them from the shadows. It was as if the forest itself was guiding them, showing them the way forward.

They came across more ancient stone pillars, each one covered in the same intricate carvings they had seen before. The symbols on the pillars glowed faintly, their light guiding them through the dense underbrush.

"This forest is incredible," Katie said, her voice filled with awe as she took in the sights around them. "It's like it's alive, like it's watching over us."

Jainu nodded, his eyes scanning the trees around them. "It is alive. The magic here... it's connected to everything in the forest. We're just a part of it, a small piece of a much larger puzzle."

They continued walking, the path beneath their feet becoming more defined as they ventured deeper into the forest. The air was thick with magic, the power of the Eternal Flame pulsing around them like a living presence.

After several hours of walking, they came across a small stream, its water crystal clear and shimmering with a soft, golden light. The stream's banks were lined with flowers, their petals glowing in the sunlight, and the air was filled with the gentle sound of the water flowing over the rocks.

Jainu and Katie knelt by the stream, their hands cupped to drink the cool, refreshing water. As they drank, they felt the magic of the forest flowing through them, filling them with a sense of peace and renewal.

"This water... it's like nothing I've ever tasted before," Katie said, her voice filled with wonder. "It's like it's alive, filled with the magic of the forest."

Jainu nodded, feeling the same sense of awe. "It is. This whole forest... it's alive, filled with magic. And we're a part of it now."

They continued on, following the stream as it wound its way through the forest. The path was lined with more flowers, their petals glowing in the sunlight, and the air was filled with the scent of blooming blossoms.

As they walked, they noticed more signs of the forest's magic. They came

across a grove of trees, their trunks twisted and gnarled, their branches intertwined to form a dense canopy overhead. The light filtering through the leaves cast a soft, golden glow over the grove, and the air was filled with the scent of pine and earth.

In the center of the grove stood a small stone altar, similar to the ones they had seen before, but this one was different. The altar was covered in intricate carvings, the symbols glowing faintly in the dim light. The air around the altar was thick with magic, and Jainu and Katie could feel its power resonating in the air around them.

They approached the altar cautiously, their steps slow and reverent. The magic here was strong, more powerful than anything they had felt before, and they knew that they were standing in a place of great significance.

"This altar... it feels different from the others," Katie said, her voice hushed. "The magic here is stronger, more intense."

Jainu nodded, feeling the same sense of awe. "It's like the forest is guiding us here, showing us something important."

As they stood before the altar, the symbols began to glow brighter, their light spreading out in ripples across the surface of the stone. The air around them hummed with energy, and Jainu could feel the magic of the forest resonating with the altar, unlocking the ancient power that lay within.

For a moment, they stood in silence, the light from the symbols surrounding them, the magic of the altar flowing through them. It was a moment of pure connection, of unity with the forest and its ancient power.

Then, as the light began to fade, Jainu and Katie opened their eyes, their hearts still filled with the warmth of the magic. The crystal in Jainu's hand was now cool, its light dimmed, but the connection they felt with the Eternal Flame remained strong.

"Do you think the magic will guide us to where we need to go next?" Katie asked, her voice filled with wonder.

Jainu nodded, his gaze still on the altar. "I believe so. This forest... it's more than just a place. It's like a living entity, and it wants to protect its secrets. But now that we've unlocked this part of its magic, I think it will guide us to the next step."

Katie smiled, her heart swelling with the possibilities of what lay ahead. "I can't wait to see what comes next."

As they left the grove and continued their journey, they felt a renewed sense of purpose. The forest was alive with magic, and they were connected to it in a way that few had ever been. The path before them was long and filled with unknown challenges, but they knew they would face whatever came their way together.

Chapter 7

The Final Convergence

The Tower of Trials

The ancient tower loomed over Jainu and Katie as they approached its dark, foreboding entrance. The air around them was thick with tension, and the ominous silence was broken only by the distant rumble of thunder. The tower was an imposing structure, its walls covered in ancient runes that seemed to pulse with a life of their own.

"This is it," Jainu muttered, his voice barely audible. "The final trial."

Katie nodded, her eyes fixed on the tower's entrance. "I feel like the tower is watching us, judging us."

As they stepped closer, the massive stone doors creaked open, revealing a dimly lit hallway. The walls inside were lined with carvings of battles, sacrifices, and ancient rituals, each telling a story of those who had come before them. Jainu couldn't shake the feeling that the tower was alive, that it was aware of their every move.

They moved cautiously through the hallway, the only sound being the soft echo of their footsteps. The air grew colder, and the flickering torches on the walls cast eerie shadows that danced around them.

"This place feels like a tomb," Katie whispered. "Like we're walking into the heart of darkness."

Jainu tightened his grip on his sword. "Stay close. We don't know what we'll face here."

The hallway opened into a vast chamber, at the center of which stood a stone altar. Surrounding the altar were three large mirrors, each reflecting a distorted image of the room. The air was thick with a sense of foreboding.

"This must be the first trial," Katie said, her voice trembling slightly. "But what are we supposed to do?"

Jainu approached the mirrors cautiously. As he stood before the first one, his reflection began to warp and twist, showing him as a younger man, full of ambition but plagued by fear. The mirror reflected his failures, his regrets, and the moments that had haunted him for years.

The scene in the mirror shifted, showing him on a battlefield, surrounded by the bodies of his fallen comrades. The weight of their deaths pressed down on him, suffocating him with guilt.

"You failed them," a voice whispered from the mirror. "You let them die because you were too weak."

Jainu's reflection sneered at him. "You're still that same scared boy, afraid of making mistakes, afraid of failing again."

Jainu clenched his fists, his heart pounding in his chest. "I've learned from my failures. I won't let them define me."

The reflection laughed, a cold, hollow sound. "Words are easy, but actions speak louder. Prove it."

The mirror shattered, and the shards reformed into a battlefield. Jainu found himself standing amidst the carnage, the weight of his comrades' deaths pressing down on him once more. But this time, he wasn't alone. Katie appeared beside him, her presence a steadying force.

"We're in this together," she said firmly. "We face this trial together."

As they moved through the battlefield, the fallen soldiers rose, their eyes glowing with a cold, eerie light. They were manifestations of Jainu's guilt, his regrets given form. The air was thick with tension as the soldiers advanced, their faces twisted in anger and pain.

Jainu felt the weight of their stares, each one a reminder of his perceived failures. The ground beneath his feet felt unstable, like it might give way at any moment. His breath came in shallow gasps, his heart pounding in his chest. But Katie's presence beside him gave him strength, her unwavering belief in him a lifeline in the sea of doubt.

"These aren't real," Katie reminded him, her voice cutting through the oppressive silence. "They're shadows, echoes of the past. They can't hurt us unless we let them."

Jainu nodded, steeling himself. He raised his sword, the blade gleaming in the dim light. "This is my past," he said, his voice steady. "But it doesn't control my future."

With a fierce battle cry, Jainu charged forward, his sword cutting through the shadowy figures. Each swing was a release, a catharsis, as he fought not just the manifestations of his guilt, but the guilt itself. The shadows hissed and writhed as they were struck, dissipating into the air like smoke.

Katie moved beside him, her own weapon flashing as she fought off the figures that approached from the other side. Her movements were fluid, confident, each strike precise and deadly. Together, they fought as one, their movements synchronized, their resolve unshakable.

The battlefield began to shift, the shadows growing thinner, weaker. The oppressive weight in the air began to lift, and the ground beneath their feet solidified. Jainu could feel the power of the tower weakening as they pushed back the darkness, reclaiming their strength.

Finally, the last of the shadows fell, its form dissolving into the air. The battlefield was silent once more, the ground littered with the remains of Jainu's past fears. He stood there, breathing heavily, his sword lowered at his side. The reflection in the mirror was gone, replaced by his true self—stronger, more resolved.

Katie placed a hand on his shoulder, her touch warm and reassuring. "You did it, Jainu. You faced your past and overcame it."

Jainu nodded, a sense of peace settling over him. "We did it. I couldn't have done it without you."

The mirror before them shimmered, and the battlefield dissolved, leaving them standing once again in the chamber. The oppressive atmosphere was gone, replaced by a sense of calm, of acceptance. The trial had tested them, but they had emerged stronger.

The next mirror called to Katie, its surface rippling as she approached. Jainu stayed close, ready to support her through whatever trials awaited. As she stepped in front of the mirror, her reflection began to change, showing her as a child, standing alone in a dark, empty room. Her small figure was dwarfed by the shadows around her, and her eyes were wide with fear.

"I remember this," Katie whispered, her voice trembling slightly. "I was always afraid of the dark when I was little. I used to think that the shadows were alive, that they would come and take me away."

The scene in the mirror shifted, showing Katie as a young girl, huddled in a corner, her arms wrapped around her knees. She was trembling, her eyes squeezed shut as she tried to block out the darkness.

"I was so scared," Katie said, her voice trembling. "But I didn't tell anyone. I didn't want them to think I was weak."

The reflection in the mirror seemed to grow darker, the shadows lengthening, creeping closer to the young Katie in the scene. The air grew colder, the darkness more suffocating.

Jainu reached out, his voice gentle. "Katie, you're not that scared little girl anymore. You've faced so much and come out stronger each time. You don't have to be afraid of the dark—or anything else—anymore."

Katie took a deep breath, her eyes fixed on the mirror. "You're right. I'm not that little girl anymore. I'm stronger than this."

The scene in the mirror shifted again, showing Katie as a young woman, standing on a cliff's edge, the wind whipping through her hair. She was alone, but there was no fear in her eyes—only determination.

"I remember this too," Katie said, her voice steadier now. "I was older, and I had finally decided to face my fear of heights. I climbed to the top of that cliff and stood there, daring myself to jump into the water below."

The reflection showed Katie taking a deep breath, then leaping off the cliff, her body slicing through the air before plunging into the water below. When she resurfaced, her face was lit with triumph and relief.

"That was the moment I realized I could face my fears," Katie said, her eyes bright with the memory. "That I didn't have to be afraid anymore."

The mirror's surface rippled once more, and Katie's reflection returned to her current self—a woman who had faced her fears, who had grown stronger and more confident with each challenge.

The light in the room grew brighter, the tension easing as the mirrors returned to their original state. The air was filled with a sense of calm, of acceptance. They had faced their fears, acknowledged their pasts, and emerged stronger.

The Guardians of the Tower

As the chamber around them began to shift again, the walls melted away to reveal a new path leading deeper into the tower. The air grew warmer, the light brighter, as they followed the path to the next trial.

The corridor they entered was different from the others. It was lined with statues of warriors, each one frozen in a pose of battle. The statues were lifelike, their expressions fierce and determined. Jainu couldn't shake the feeling that they were being watched.

"These statues," Katie murmured, running her fingers along the cold stone. "They're not just art. They're the guardians of the tower."

Jainu frowned. "Guardians? You mean these statues..."

Katie nodded. "They were once like us—warriors who came to the tower to prove themselves. But they failed, and now they stand as eternal sentinels, guarding the tower from those who would follow in their footsteps."

As they moved deeper into the corridor, the statues seemed to come to life. The air crackled with energy, and the statues' eyes began to glow with a faint light. The ground trembled beneath their feet, and the statues slowly turned their heads to watch Jainu and Katie as they passed.

"This is their trial," Jainu said, his voice tense. "They failed, but we won't. We can't."

Katie glanced at him, her eyes filled with determination. "We'll make it through this. Together."

The corridor led to a large, circular chamber, the walls lined with even more statues. In the center of the room stood a massive stone pedestal, upon which rested a glowing crystal. The air was thick with magic, and the energy in the room was almost palpable.

"This must be the heart of the tower," Katie said, her voice filled with awe. "The crystal—it's the source of the tower's power."

As they approached the pedestal, the statues around the room began to move, their stone limbs creaking as they came to life. The guardians stepped down from their pedestals, their movements slow and deliberate, their eyes fixed on Jainu and Katie.

"We have to protect the crystal," one of the guardians said, its voice a low, rumbling echo. "It must not fall into the hands of the unworthy."

Jainu drew his sword, his heart pounding in his chest. "We're not here to take the crystal. We're here to prove ourselves, just like you once were."

The guardian shook its head, its expression grim. "We failed our trial, and now we are bound to this place, forever guarding the crystal. If you wish to pass, you must prove your worth."

The other guardians stepped forward, their weapons drawn. The air in the room grew colder, and the ground beneath their feet seemed to pulse with energy.

"We won't fail," Katie said, her voice steady. "We're ready for this."

The guardians attacked with a speed and strength that belied their stone forms. Jainu and Katie moved as one, their weapons flashing in the dim light as they fought off the relentless assault. The guardians were powerful, their movements precise and calculated, but Jainu and Katie had faced many battles together, and their bond was stronger than any stone.

The battle raged on, the air filled with the sound of clashing steel and the crackle of magic. Jainu felt the weight of the fight pressing down on him, the exhaustion creeping into his limbs, but he pushed forward, determined to prove himself worthy.

Katie fought beside him, her movements graceful and fluid, her strikes deadly accurate. She could feel the energy of the tower pulsing around them, the magic almost alive as it tested their resolve.

Finally, with a final, desperate surge of strength, they drove back the last of the guardians. The statues crumbled to the ground, their stone forms breaking apart as the magic that animated them faded away.

The chamber fell silent, the only sound their labored breathing. The crystal on the pedestal glowed brighter, its light filling the room with a warm, soothing energy.

"You have proven yourselves," the voice of the first guardian echoed through the chamber, though the statue had crumbled. "The crystal is yours to command. Use its power wisely."

Jainu and Katie approached the pedestal, their hearts pounding with a mixture of relief and anticipation. They had passed the trial, but the journey was not yet over.

As they reached out to touch the crystal, the air around them shimmered, and the room began to dissolve. The walls of the chamber melted away, revealing a new path that led deeper into the heart of the tower.

The Final Trial – The Keeper of the Flame

The door swung open with a deep, resonant creak, revealing a vast, circular chamber beyond. The air inside was thick with the scent of incense and something else—something ancient and powerful, like the lingering echo of a long-forgotten spell. The chamber was dimly lit by a series of torches that lined the walls, their flames flickering with an otherworldly blue light.

At the center of the chamber stood a massive figure, cloaked in shadows. The figure's presence was overwhelming, filling the room with an oppressive energy that made the air feel heavy, almost suffocating. Jainu and Katie could feel the power radiating from the figure, a force of pure magic that resonated with the very stone of the tower.

"This must be the Keeper," Katie whispered, her voice trembling with a mixture of fear and awe. "The final guardian of the Eternal Flame."

Jainu nodded, his hand tightening around the hilt of his sword. "We need to be ready for anything. This is the last trial, and it won't be easy."

The Keeper stepped forward, its form shifting and solidifying as it emerged from the shadows. It was tall, taller than any human, and its body was cloaked in dark, flowing robes that seemed to absorb the light. Its face was hidden beneath a hood, but its eyes glowed with a deep, otherworldly light that pierced the darkness.

"You have come far, travelers," the Keeper said, its voice echoing through the chamber like the tolling of a great bell. "You have faced many trials, but your journey ends here. Only one who is truly worthy can command the power of the Eternal Flame."

Jainu and Katie exchanged a glance, their hearts pounding with anticipation. They had known that the final trial would be a battle, but the Keeper's presence was more formidable than they had anticipated.

"We're ready," Jainu said, his voice steady despite the tension in the air.

Katie nodded, her gaze fixed on the shadowy figure. "We've come too far to turn back now."

The Keeper raised its hand, and the air around them crackled with energy. The shadows in the room began to shift and twist, coalescing into the forms of dark, twisted creatures—beasts of shadow and smoke, their eyes glowing with a malevolent light.

"These are the guardians of the Flame," the Keeper said, its voice filled with ancient authority. "To reach the Flame, you must first defeat them."

The creatures lunged at them, their movements quick and erratic. Jainu and Katie leapt into action, their weapons flashing in the dim light as they fought back the shadowy beasts. The battle was intense, the air filled with the clash of steel and the crackle of magic as they struggled to hold their ground.

Jainu moved with precision, his sword cutting through the shadows with deadly accuracy. Each strike was deliberate, each movement calculated to counter the creatures' unpredictable attacks. He had faced many battles before, but the Keeper's guardians were unlike anything he had encountered—creatures born of darkness and magic, their forms constantly shifting and changing.

Katie fought beside him, her movements fluid and graceful as she deflected the creatures' attacks. She could feel the weight of the magic in the air, the oppressive energy that seemed to fuel the creatures' relentless assault. But she refused to give in, her determination driving her forward even as the battle raged around her.

The creatures were relentless, their attacks growing more frenzied as the battle wore on. Jainu and Katie found themselves pushed to their limits, their strength waning as they struggled to keep the creatures at bay.

"We can't keep this up much longer," Katie panted, her breath coming in ragged gasps.

"We have to," Jainu replied, his voice filled with grim determination. "We're almost there."

With a final surge of effort, they drove back the last of the creatures, their forms dissipating into the air like smoke. The chamber fell silent, the only sound their labored breathing as they stood over the remains of the defeated guardians.

The Keeper watched them, its eyes glowing with a cold, calculating light. "You have proven your strength, your resolve. But strength alone is not enough to command the power of the Eternal Flame."

The Keeper raised its hand again, and the chamber began to shift. The floor beneath their feet trembled, and the walls seemed to melt away, revealing a new chamber beyond. This one was smaller, more intimate, with walls lined with mirrors that reflected their images back at them from every angle.

"This is the final trial," the Keeper said, its voice filled with a quiet intensity. "The trial of the heart. To command the Flame, you must confront the truth of who you are."

Jainu and Katie exchanged a glance, their hearts pounding with a mixture of fear and anticipation. They had faced many challenges, but this... this was different. This was a test of their very souls.

Taking a deep breath, they stepped forward, each of them standing before a mirror. For a moment, all they saw were their own reflections, but then, the images began to change.

Jainu's reflection shifted to show him standing alone, surrounded by the bodies of those he had failed to protect. The guilt and shame he had carried for so long rose up, a dark tide that threatened to overwhelm him. He saw the faces of those he had lost, the weight of their deaths pressing down on him like a physical force.

Katie's mirror showed her surrounded by shadows, the darkness closing in on her as she struggled to find a way out. She saw the moments of doubt, the times she had questioned her own worth, the fear that she wasn't strong enough, wasn't good enough, to protect those she loved.

The mirrors showed them their deepest fears, their darkest moments, the parts of themselves they had tried to bury and forget. The air grew colder, the darkness in the room thickening as the images became more intense, more vivid.

"We have to face this," Jainu said, his voice trembling as he forced himself to look at the mirror. "We have to accept it."

Katie nodded, her heart pounding as she stared into the depths of the mirror. "We can't change the past, but we can learn from it. We can be stronger because of it."

The images in the mirrors flickered, the darkness beginning to recede as they spoke. The reflections of their fears, their doubts, began to fade, replaced by the images of who they had become. Jainu saw himself standing tall, a leader who had learned from his mistakes, who had found strength in his vulnerability. Katie saw herself as a protector, someone who had faced her fears and emerged stronger, someone who had learned to trust in her own strength.

The light in the room grew brighter, the tension easing as the mirrors returned to their original state. The air was filled with a sense of calm, of acceptance. They had faced their fears, acknowledged their pasts, and emerged stronger.

As the light from the mirrors faded, the Keeper stepped forward, its form solidifying as it approached them. "You have faced your fears, confronted the truth of who you are. You have proven yourselves worthy."

The Keeper reached out, placing a hand on each of their shoulders. "The power of the Eternal Flame is not just a tool to be wielded—it is a responsibility, a burden, and a gift. You must choose how you will use this power, knowing that your decision will shape the future of this world."

Jainu and Katie exchanged a glance, their hearts swelling with a mixture of pride and humility. They had come so far, faced so much, and now, standing at the threshold of power, they knew the weight of the choice before them.

"We will use the power to protect this world," Jainu said, his voice steady. "To ensure that it remains safe from those who would seek to harm it."

Katie nodded in agreement. "We will guard the Flame and use its magic to heal and to help those in need."

The Keeper's eyes glowed with approval. "Then you have made your choice. The power of the Eternal Flame is now yours to command. Use it wisely, for it is a force that can create or destroy, depending on how it is wielded."

As the Keeper spoke, the room around them began to glow with a brilliant light. The energy of the Eternal Flame surged through them, filling them with a sense of purpose, of unity. They could feel the magic flowing through their veins, connecting them to the very heart of the world.

The Keeper stepped back, its form beginning to fade as the light intensified. "Remember, travelers, the power of the Flame is yours, but it comes with great responsibility. Guard it well, and let it guide you on your journey."

With those final words, the Keeper disappeared, leaving Jainu and Katie standing alone in the chamber. The light from the mirrors dimmed, but the connection they felt with the Eternal Flame remained strong.

"We did it," Katie whispered, her voice filled with awe. "We unlocked the power of the Eternal Flame."

Jainu nodded, his heart pounding with a mixture of excitement and awe. "But this is just the beginning. There's so much more to discover, so much more to learn."

Katie looked at him, her eyes filled with determination. "Then let's keep going. Let's find out what the Eternal Flame has in store for us."

They turned toward the door that had appeared at the far end of the chamber, a sense of purpose guiding their steps. They had faced their fears, unlocked the magic of the tower, and emerged stronger, more united.

As they stepped through the door, the light from the mirrors dimmed, but the connection they felt with the Eternal Flame remained strong. The path ahead was long and winding, but they were no longer afraid. The magic of the Eternal Flame was alive within them, guiding them toward the future.

Epilogue

A New Dawn

The first light of dawn filtered through the dense canopy of the ancient forest, casting a soft, golden glow over the landscape. The air was crisp and cool, carrying with it the fresh scent of earth and pine. The world seemed to be holding its breath, as if aware that something monumental had just occurred.

Jainu and Katie stood at the edge of the clearing, looking out over the rolling hills that stretched into the horizon. The journey they had embarked on together, the trials they had faced, and the battles they had fought were all behind them now, but the weight of their experiences lingered.

"It's hard to believe it's over," Katie said softly, her eyes tracing the path they had taken through the forest. "After everything we've been through, it almost feels... surreal."

Jainu nodded, his gaze fixed on the distant mountains. The Eternal Flame, a source of immense power and responsibility, now resided within them. Its warmth pulsed in his chest, a constant reminder of the burden they had accepted. "It is surreal. But it's also a beginning—a new chapter in our lives."

Katie turned to face him, a small smile playing on her lips. "A new chapter with new challenges, no doubt. But at least we'll face them together."

Jainu met her gaze, a sense of peace settling over him. They had grown closer during their journey, their bond forged in the fires of battle and the depths of the tower's trials. Katie's optimism and unwavering determination had been a light in the darkness, guiding him when he had faltered. And in turn, he had found strength in her presence, discovering facets of himself that he had long thought lost.

"We're stronger now," Jainu said, his voice filled with quiet resolve. "Whatever comes next, we're ready for it."

Katie reached out, taking his hand in hers. "We have to be. The world won't wait for us to catch our breath. But for now... let's take a moment to appreciate this. We've earned it."

They stood there in silence for a while, watching as the sun slowly climbed higher in the sky, painting the landscape in warm hues of gold and orange. The tranquility of the moment was a stark contrast to the chaos they had endured, a reminder that peace could be found even in the aftermath of the storm.

As the sun continued its ascent, Jainu felt a stirring in his chest, a gentle urging from the Eternal Flame. The power within him was vast and ancient, but it was also patient, waiting for them to decide how best to wield it. There was a world beyond the horizon that needed their help, and the responsibilities they had taken on were not to be ignored.

"Katie," Jainu began, his voice thoughtful, "what do you think we should do next? The world is full of places that could benefit from the Flame's power. We could help so many people."

Katie squeezed his hand, her expression turning serious. "I've been thinking about that too. There are kingdoms torn apart by war, villages suffering from famine, and places where magic has been corrupted. We have the power to make a real difference, to bring hope to those who need it most."

Jainu nodded. "Then that's what we'll do. We'll use the Flame to heal, to protect, and to bring balance back to the world. But we'll do it on our terms, and we'll make sure we stay true to who we are."

Katie smiled, a spark of excitement in her eyes. "It won't be easy, but nothing worth doing ever is. And besides, I have a feeling we're going to have a lot of fun along the way."

Jainu chuckled, a genuine smile spreading across his face. "Fun, huh? I suppose we could use a little more of that after everything."

Katie's expression softened as she looked out at the horizon once more. "We've faced the darkness together, and now we get to bring a little light into the world. I think that's a pretty good way to spend our lives, don't you?"

Jainu squeezed her hand in return, feeling a warmth in his heart that rivaled the power of the Flame itself. "I couldn't agree more."

With a shared sense of purpose, they turned away from the clearing and began their journey anew. The path before them was uncertain, filled with both danger and opportunity, but they were no longer afraid. Together, they had faced their deepest fears and emerged stronger, united by a bond that could not be broken.

As they walked side by side, the sun climbed higher in the sky, bathing the world in its radiant light. The shadows of the past were behind them, and a new dawn had begun—a dawn filled with promise, with hope, and with the certainty that whatever challenges lay ahead, they would face them together.

And so, with the Eternal Flame as their guide, Jainu and Katie set forth into the world, ready to shape its future with courage, compassion, and the unbreakable strength of their friendship.

The adventure was far from over, but for now, they embraced the journey with open hearts and unwavering resolve, knowing that the greatest challenges often brought the most profound rewards.